TAVERN TALES

AN ARKLE WRIGHT SHORT STORY COLLECTION

RAYMOND S FLEX

CONTENTS

MORNING PEOPLE

1

LET ME GIVE YOU a tip for your next holiday in the Fritten System—steer yourself well clear of Telfon-90. I'll say that again for the benefit of you lot at the back: For the love of God, steer clear of Telfon-90.

Just my luck that the *Navaplastas*—my pride and joy, my whole damn life—decided to poot itself out just as I skirted the rings of Telfon. As much as I love the *Nava* I have to admit that it happens one heck of a bunch of times. She's not exactly the most reliable ship in the galaxy, but—as I might've said once or twice before—don't tell her you heard me saying that: she's got a pretty mean temper on her for a hunk of wires and metal.

And so, eyeing that damn readout, those pissing awful numbers telling me that there was no pressure in some-such piece of equipment I didn't know the location of—let alone its name or what the hell it did—I found the *Nava* losing power fast.

That was the upshot of the matter.

Whatever that piece of crap was, it meant one thing and one thing only: I had to park up and go find a mechanic. That, I guess right there's one of the disadvantages of being a solo-flyer, and being a numbnuts like me. It's maybe not much of an exaggeration that I'd need some sort of direction to sort my arse my elbow. All right, I could probably find my arse easily enough, the elbow, well, let's just say that it's smothered between a pair of mounds of fat.

We plummeted down through the atmosphere, as only a petered-out spaceship can do, which is to say that we were caught in a flat spin, smoke pouring out of every damn orifice it seemed. I wrestled with those controls, sweating, cursing—mainly cursing—and tried to find some semblance of direction, to at least get us pointing at a sea.

. . . if this planet had any sea.

There was a nice positive thought breaking out in my head, as I swore myself blind, given that I'd expected us to burn up in the atmosphere—I'd thought that whatever had broke in the ship might've taken the force fields down with it. Now, though, I found myself facing up to another tricky situation, although something vaguely in my control. I guessed to be about one klick from smashing up on the surface, which was quickly coming into focus down below, through matted grey cloud.

My harness dug into my flesh, my shoulders, neck—those ankle ones I'd had put fresh on about a week back—and I felt all the air leaving my lungs as I yanked back on the control stick, attempting to bring that nose back up, to get us pointed in some sort of horizontal direction. But no, the *Nava*—bless her—wasn't in anything like a cooperative mood. And so I did whatever any good smuggler does—anyone who doesn't know the first thing about spaceships, or how the *hell* they operate, and I pressed every damn button in front of me.

Oh, this was a real press-a-thon, let me tell you. I got those porky fingertips rushing over those buttons, I was pulling levers, I even turned a couple of knobs. And you know what? That damn panic only worked!

As I leaned back into my chair, yanking on the control stick as hard as I possibly could, I found it gaining some purchase, the nose was tilting its way up, coming back up—as in going up vertically. If I'd known any sort of uplifting songs—not those sodden moiser shanties I sing with the boys down *The Bitch's Leap*—I would've sung them. So since it appeared my repertoire was lacking I settled on a fairly upbeat, *"Yippee!"*

I soon got myself back under control, though, because the simple fact of the matter was that the *Nava*—bless her again—was simply shunting her way along, coasting I think's the technical term and, without being too rude to the people of Telfon-90, there was a dirty great, shitty lake right below.

Now, being a smuggler I've got the *Nava* into some ugly spots, but, *come on*, a lake of shit? As a captain you've gotta set some boundaries for your big girl, or maybe she won't love you no more.

And so, *coasting* along, through the air, I wrestled with that control stick, bringing us in—to my delight—over that shitty lake, and to what looked like a much more promising patch of sand. Actually, as we tore on, I noticed that this thing was big, in fact it looked like a whole damn desert.

We passed over the dunes, me still struggling to keep the *Nava* from doing a nosedive—one of her best tricks—and trying to pick out a nice spot to land, somewhere I could be reasonably sure we weren't going to sink into some quicksand, if that even exists. I focussed on a spot that looked just about as nice as we were going to find, given the circumstances, and I banked sharp to the left, bringing us down between a pair of dunes, in a relatively flat spot.

I guess that maybe a while back—many moons ago when I was a cadet in the FSA, that's the Fritten Space Authorities for the uninitiated, basically the Space Police—I might've taken some class on emergency landings, probably had a whole instructor, maybe a freaking exam for all I remember. All I know is that, then, when I brought the *Nava* in it was with an almighty *bump*. No this wasn't just a *bump*, that's not the right word. What this was, well, it was a *damn* big *bump*.

Maybe my steering could've been a little better. The *Nava* hit the sand at about forty-five degrees, her left side getting buried almost right away. Sand flew up against the front windows, and I listened to that grainy *rustle* of sand getting into all sorts of places that it's probably not meant to get into in spaceships. Even I know the importance of not sticking stuff in engines, or exhausts, or whatever. Just as you wouldn't stick stuff . . . oh, you get my meaning.

I guess I must've blacked out for a few moments, at least I seemed to forget just about everything when I recall hearing the communicator humming away to itself. If there's one thing I've noticed about phone calls it's that they damn well come whenever they please: when you're brushing your teeth, on the can . . . or crashing into deserts.

I uncurled a flimsy arm and reached out to tap the button—it's one of the few buttons in the ship that I know, without a doubt, what it does. There was a voice on the other end, someone nearby, someone wanting to *help* me out. Now, I'm into people being kind and all that, but there's really one thing that rankles a smuggler, one thing that he will hold onto till the last gasp of air has leaked from his lungs, and that's his autonomy, dammit, we hate to give up that blessed autonomy. Really it comes down to one thing above all others and it's really the fact that you just don't want people poking about your ship, all nosey and the like. It's a smuggler's job to keep whatever he's packing a hushed-up secret. And then come times like these, like when you've just crashed into a strange planet and your ship's singing all sorts of notes you never even knew existed, and you've just got to roll with the punches.

So I rolled with the punches.

2

NEXT THING I KNEW I was waking up in the dark, in a bed, a pretty neatly made bed—sheets tucked in around the edges, that sort of deal—and my brain felt like it was trying to bash its way out of my skull with a blunt instrument . . . although I guess there're some that'd say my brain *is* a blunt instrument.

The room wasn't all that large. Just a chest of drawers across from me—a smooth, *ersatz* pine effort no doubt imported in from somewhere in the Barnes System, known for its well-made, and economical, knockoffs. There was a window too, but that wasn't up to all that much, what with the blind drawn down, leaving the place in a steady gloom.

My migraine ratcheted up a couple of notches so I had to squeeze my eyes shut with the pain of it all. As I eased myself down from that penetrating, unceasing agony, I made out the light sounds of footsteps, carrying down the hall. I turned my attention to the door—one of those slick sliding models . . . all right, they're not all that slick, but there are some colonies that don't even have doors, for Christ's sake.

The doorknob rotated and light just poured into the damn room—just that overpowering daylight that literally forces you to drag that bedcover up and drape it over your eyes, which was what I did them. As I lay under that sheet, I thought to myself, *Morning people, just what in hell's name have I got myself into here?*

A young lady, blond hair down to her arse, a nice powder blue dress which swept her ankles, carried a tray into the room. She glanced over at me briefly, gave me a crisp smile that damn near sent me back beneath those bed sheets shivering. It was that bright. When she spoke, her voice was thick as treacle, and twice as sticky. In fact, I started rethinking her age because, man, that was *not* the voice of a twenty-something girl—she had to be at least forty, fifty maybe. "Captain Wright? Are you awake?"

Now, I'm not all that good at the best of times, but in the morning, that's a whole different matter. A whole different planet. I grumbled to myself then said, rubbing my eyelids with my stubby fingers, "How'd you know my name?"

"Your distress signal," she said. "Our terminal intercepted it."

"I didn't send no *distress* signal," I said, taking extra-special delight in slithering on the word 'distress.'

Then I got a better grip on myself, actually managed to hoik myself up into some kind of sitting position, if you can believe that. Still with my hand gingerly in the general space of my eyes, I continued, "You actually have a *damn* terminal out here?"

She smiled lightly, the kind that you give to a guest who's most likely a fastidious neighbour—you know, someone who just *pops up* wherever and whenever, but, for the sake of tranquillity, you gotta live with them. Yeah, that was her smile. Do I blame her? No, not in the slightest. "Captain Wright," she said.

"Arkle," I said, rubbing my head, and wondering how badly the air must stink in the room, what with my personal hygiene levels having reached an all-time low that week—truth be told I couldn't remember my last shower, maybe I should've taken a picture to remind myself, something to get all dewy-eyed and nostalgic over.

"Right," she said, and then, "*Arkle,*" as if I was speaking anything else other than Basic. "Your ship—"

That caught my attention, a jolt of electricity leaping up my spine. I guessed I looked something akin to a mother who's just heard her toddler's been walking about all over a drone motorway. "The *Navaplastas*," I said. "How in the hell is she?"

Again, this woman—this too-good-to-be-true angel—blasted me with her pearly whites. "Our mechanics are taking care of your ship. They should have the repairs done soon."

That gave me another jolt. Just as I said before, if there's one thing a smuggler prides himself on it's not letting any sticky fingers within shouting distance of his ship—and, oh my, do mechanics have sticky fingers . . .

She seemed to sense my panic and laid her hand on my leg, still covered by the bed sheet. I have to admit that I did get another little tingle, and this time—first time in a long time—it had nothing to do with the *Navaplastas*. "The ship will be fine, captain. You just relax. Take your time. You're still in shock following the crash."

"Where am I?" I said, berating myself for not having asked such a simple question earlier—I guess a man's got his priorities.

"New Burton."

"New Burton? What the hell's that?"

"It's a village, *our* village. We live a little way out from the central colonies here—just our little patch. You know, you were awfully lucky to land close by here. There's an awful lot of nothing on this planet and you just managed to pick a civilised part."

"Yeah," I said, already eyeing up my breakfast tray—all that shock just about seeping away now, and my appetite very much returning. I eyed that glass of freshly squeezed orange juice, smelled those rashers of bacon—not *ersatz*, the real thing—and that egg, and *those* beans.

My stomach wobbled.

"Well," she said, removing her hand from its, not unwelcome, place on my leg, "I'll leave you to sleep a while. All you've to do is call out if you need something."

"Right," I said, already shifting my increasingly horrendous bulk over toward my breakfast tray. "Got it, listen, thanks . . . thanks for all this."

She lingered in the doorway, that same stiff smile spreading her cheeks. "Don't mention it, captain."

And then I tucked into that breakfast big time.

3

ALL RIGHT, I might be a slob who likes his sleep too much, but I do have one policy that I've stuck to over the years and that's *Once I'm up, I'm up.*

No questions.

No *naps*.

I'm determined to stay on my feet or—as is usually the case—at the controls till my head literally lulls forward onto my chest and that honey-sweet sleep catches me out. And, most certainly, I do not like sleeping in when I'm a guest in someone's house—and so I draped my stained jacket over my shoulders, fastened on my trousers—already feeling a touch of sympathy for whoever suffered the great indignity of undressing me in the first place—and plunged my chubby calves down, right down, into my stonking smuggler's boots, those same boots which make me feel just about ten feet tall.

They *do* have a heel on them, that's for certain.

Next up was the question of navigating a stranger's house—again something which, as a smuggler, I should have no qualms about, after all I'm lewd, crude and, on occasion, awfully sweary, and yet I did feel a little awkward skulking about someone else's home, I suppose rationalising it as the same way I'd feel with some numbnuts skulking around the *Nava*.

The house itself was built on a single storey, as is the case with a lot of these colonial upstarts—they start simple before building on it, and inevitably heading on down the path of becoming a mega city.

And the place was just so light—couldn't get over that at all. Not just the amount of windows, but every last little thing was painted white—white walls, white carpets, white ceiling, white-painted doors.

Man, I wondered if these people *shitted* white.

The air smelled of some flowers or other, and there was a stench of furniture polish which clung to everything. I wandered on along the hall, to the kitchen, which was just as deserted as the rest of the house—and I was kinda glad not having to suffer an awkward introduction, 'Hey, I'm the guy you peeled out of his tin can last night, you know, the one who's been stinking out your guest room?'

Yeah, I'd rather miss out on that if I possibly could.

I slipped out through the door—actually slipping on that step, it was polished within a damn inch of its life—and then piled out along the garden path, taking in the primly trimmed bushes, the lush carpet of grass, cut at that perfect an inch-and-a-half length— that was a whole other *long* conversation in another system, thankfully faraway. Out through the gate I went, and into the street.

Well, it wasn't hard to work out where my ship was kept, since there was a sheening white dome at the end of the road, about a hundred yards away—the terminal. And so I did what I have loathed to do ever since I started out on this smuggling lark: walk.

One foot in front of the other, the sweats already coming raining down. I glanced up, straining in the light from whatever the local star was, to see the artificial atmosphere—the bubble covering us all—like a razor-thin plastic wrapping. Never could get the hang of why people would want to live under those things. But, then again, I suppose they were *morning people*.

On my way to the terminal something happened that doesn't usually when I'm on my way to retrieve the *Nava* from whatever thankless situation I've got her all tangled in. There was a small hut, nothing more than a few planks of wood—despite its fairly shabby appearance it looked to be that good quality imitation stuff that pine chest of drawers back in the bedroom was made of. Again, unlike the norm, I found myself pretty intrigued stumbling upon this out-of-place blot on the otherwise pristine piece of real estate that was New Burton. And so, pretty unlike me, I shifted off the neat concrete road and crunched over the uneven dirt to this shack.

Just as I got about ten, fifteen paces away, I heard the sound of humming, that unmistakable sound of some computer—don't get me started on pissing computers—whirring away inside. Should've known better then, I guessed, should've just walked away. But now that I'd gone to all that effort, no doubt burning my way into one of my well-won pounds of fat, I made the final few steps and peeled back the door.

Inside there was a lift shaft. That was all. A plain lift shaft nestled inside.

I shrugged to myself and gazed down there. And what I saw . . . what I think I saw, were human-sized tube upon human-sized tube of . . . well, from what I could make of it, tubes full of humans.

I sweated a little more. I glanced round, afraid someone might've snuck up on me. Still, just like before, there was no one around. And so, still with that strange new sense of intrigue flowing through my veins, I jabbed the button—waited for the rattling lift cage to wobble its way up the shaft. Then I got in and descended.

That horrible sound of shaking metal—like a pair of drone shopping trolleys meshing one into the other, that way they do to save space—accompanied my journey down into the pits of Telfon-90, down below the settlement known as New Burton. And, before I quite knew what I was sticking my large boots in, I was standing at the bottom on the shaft, staring up at those tubes .. . those tubes of humans.

Everything was set in gloom from where I stood, so—using some of the little pragmatic initiative I have—I flipped the switch beside the lift, and, low and behold, a great big dirty fluorescent bulb flickered on above, lighting up row upon row of the tubes.

Each tube had a sickly greenie-yellow liquid inside, bubbles all nestled up against the glass. And, from each, a leathery human face was pressed up against the glass. It didn't take long for me to find a familiar one—needless to say, that of my host, that blond woman who'd served me breakfast.

Now, I'm not trying to make out that I'm a hardened guy—I'm a space smuggler, read into that what you will—but I didn't freak out, or scream, even grumble. Because, and let's set this straight, after all the shit I've seen traipsing about the universe it takes quite a bit to shock me . . . even a little. What you learn, a little bit after wandering the universe, is that weird people—*morning people*, especially—find their ways into all sorts of nooks and crannies, eking themselves out a niche here, a niche there. This wasn't any different.

So I strolled my way past the tube of, what appeared to be, a slightly younger model of my host, maybe late teens, early twenties, to the end of the chamber where I found the computer.

Didn't I say that about computers? There's always a damn computer.

And, surprise, surprise, this particular *damn* computer was wired up between a pair of tubes, one of them with a walkway, an opening cut out of it, and the other, standing beside it, without an opening—what I supposed they squeezed the freshly-baked humans into. For those of you that haven't been paying attention during this story, let me spell it out to you a little clearer. There was one whacko, or potentially several *whackos*, all cooking up humans in this basement, snuggled away in the corner of the Fritten System.

Usually, in these sorts of circumstances, I get a pretty clear idea of what I'm meant to do—and that is to *get the fuck* out of there. And, please, that was just what I had in mind at that particular moment in time—in fact, I was just on the point of turning on the proverbial heel and beating my retreat for that lift shaft, when I caught sight of something familiar.

My face.

4

RIGHT, back when I said that much doesn't throw me—that's when it's not personal. To put it simply, that *did* throw me, and in a big way too. Oh, I was most likely peach-faced, stumbling all over the place like a patron freshly chucked from *The Bitch's Leap* just around midnight—and believe me, once or twice . . . all right, once or twice *dozen* . . . I have been that patron. It was a wonder I got myself back over to that lift and squeezed my gut back into that, pretty trim, lift space.

As I stood there, stewing over that revelation—literally *stewing* —I thought of my fresh face that whatever scientist they had working here had produced. They'd done nothing less than clone me—made a new, younger version of myself. I wondered how long I'd been knocked out. Had they done it quickly?—because, damn, they must've used a potato masher to get my mass into *that* tube . . . as for my younger self, I did say that I'd served in the FSA, didn't I?

I used to be quite the trim figure.

Not before time I emerged back on the surface and ran—that's R-A-N, for any of you unbelieving snickerers—and arrived at the terminal to New Burton sweating buckets and panting like a horse, an extremely out-of-shape horse.

That terminal door, why it was wide open, thank God, and it would just happen that—having seen precisely no one since prising myself up out of bed that morning—the place was occupied by three mechanics. They, each of them, were all fresh-faced, young, had meaty muscles and proud, well-shaped square chins.

All of them bore wrenches or drills or some other object that I didn't feel all that comfortable going *mano a mano* with without my trusty blaster.

Yeah, that's right, my blaster was in the blessed *Navaplastas*.

That was where my attention went next, to the *Nava*, lurking behind them, still on struts, but without any loose panels open, and—I hoped—fully operational. I saw, to my delight, that the doors remained locked. But, then again, no one has *ever* managed to breach the *Nava's* everything-proof security systems.

Damn right too, you have no idea how much I've spent on those systems over the years.

The mechanics sort of formed a circle around me, blocking both my escape and any attempted run for the *Nava*, each of them looking threatening with their assorted object, till the familiar voice—the voice from that morning—called them off. I say called them off, but they really just stopped where they were, still looking just as threatening with those blunt implements.

The blond woman appeared from out of a side room. She had that same false smile, still going at it. "Captain," she said, that *purr* to her voice still very much present. "Where do you think you're going in such a hurry?"

Now, at this point in an interaction, I'm lifting my blaster and shooting like crazy. Here, though, as I've already mentioned, that wasn't an option.

To say that I had to resort to Plan B would imply that I had any sort of structure or aim in mind with my life in general, but I suppose that my second natural reaction to threatening situations is to get lippy.

"Listen, lady, thanks for those repairs, and stuff, but now's the time for me to leave—that clone, whatever that thing is—fine, just take it, I won't begrudge you whatever DNA you've decided to wrestle from these veins, we'll call it quits."

That smile of hers widened.

I thought I felt the mechanics getting close all over again.

"I'm Doctor Tyrall," she said. "And this—*New Burton*—is my dream." She cocked her head to one side, not a little maniacally. "Didn't you notice the jammer I have under the blanket in the corner over there? The way that I brought you, that ship of yours, down here to join us?"

Now she mentioned it I did see that jammer, or what she claimed was the jammer. She was giving me an awful lot of credit—I thought—since even if I had seen what was under that blanket, I never in a million years would've seen to identifying it.

"Yes," she said. "A perfect new citizen—you'll join us here, captain. It's not every day a ship passes overhead, unregistered, unmissed anywhere else." Her features darkened. "Unfortunately for things to work out we'll need to take care of *that* body of yours —it's no good for you, all fat and gooey, we'll give you a fresh one, a new start."

Those mechanics were getting awfully close again.

"I take that as an offence," I said, not taking eyes off those mechanics. "As a matter of fact I've got not a little attached to some of these rolls of fat—sentimental value, you see."

One of the mechanics, an especially fresh-faced, firm-chinned one, swung his wrench at me, and, sticking out my pudgy arm, I caught him and jerked his arm around, using all the weight I could muster.

After a brief struggle, I got the wrench free from his vicelike grip and then just went *wild*.

I screamed out at the tops of my lungs spinning round in ever-increasingly faster circles. One thing a fat bastard like me has got is ballast. I felt that wrench make contact with those firm chins, cracking bone, sending my tormentors toppling over. I stopped, feeling my heart thudding its way up my throat, threatening to make an appearance in my mouth, and examined the scene.

All three mechanics, prostate on the floor, arms flailing out.

Knocked out cold.

I turned to Doctor Tyrall, standing there with a slight pout, a blaster pointed at my chest. "Right, captain," she said. "That was an impressive display but I think I've seen enough."

A lump formed in my throat. I swallowed it back. "Wait," I said, praying that I'd form some germ of a thought in my mind, something to strike a deal with. "I . . . I could help you, bring more people here.

"For you to *help* them."

She cocked her head even further to one side.

Looked like I was on a roll—not always as hard as it looks with these nutters. "That's right," I said. "I ain't got no job, no contract, no marks on the ship. It'd be perfect."

"And I'd pay you?"

"That'd be nice."

She turned the thought over in her mind, certainly giving it serious thought. She parted her lips, then rested her tongue on her lower lip. "I *would* appreciate some new citizens." Then she glanced back at the *Nava*. "All right," she said.

Already I made quick steps over to the *Nava*, already feeling the smoothness of that arse-groove in the captain's seat, savouring the thought.

Although I didn't turn around I felt that blaster, her aiming that thing, at my back. She added, "And, captain, don't even think of firing those weapons against New Burton—that jammer will block all signals."

"Gotcha," I said, flipping through the security protocols, then, with a sigh of relief, bursting in through the side door.

I hardly felt my feet touch the ground on my way to the cockpit, and before I knew it I was at the controls, feeling that firm control stick in my grip, firing up the engines—which snarled delectably. Without so much as a look back, I ploughed out through the hangar and out into that beautiful outside world through the slot which opened in the bubble.

Now, I did test those weapons, to see if her theory held water. And, just like she said: *no go.*

After that, well, I just shot right up into space, I'm a space smuggler after all, not some kind of goddamn saint. I promised myself that next time I shot by a drop-in implant clinic I'd get one of those laser guns melded to my arm.

Right, now *that* would be paranoid.

THE TOURIST

1

I 'D JUST ABOUT got sat down in *The Bitch's Leap* on Hortenine-6 when I saw him walking in.

I was just minding my own business, sipping away at my moiser, not really thinking about anything. There was a pair of other space smugglers sitting at my table, Drek Smutly and Lulub Flonston. Both of them had bought into that whole waistcoat fashion that was buzzing round the Fritten System, and the leather trousers to go with it.

As for me, nah, I was still rocking a pair of jeans that'd last fit me around a decade ago and my least-stained shirt—opened down to the base of my ribcage. You might gather that *The Bitch's* certainly ain't the classiest joint in the galaxy. And you'd be right about that.

Drek and Lulub were chatting about something or other, maybe about just where they'd each picked up their own waistcoats. As for me, though, I've never really given much of a shit for fashion. Way I see it, if it keeps me warm and free from the attention of whatever authorities I happen to be bumping into planetside, that's good enough for me.

I watched the guy step in through the door, and just everything about him screamed out *tourist* to me. Thinking about it now, it was most likely that suitcase he held down at his side, a brown one with scuff marks all round the edge, and with a hefty dent in it to boot. What did it, though, was probably that he was wearing shorts then sandals with socks, the socks hoiked up to just about where his calves started.

Neither Drek or Lulub noticed the tourist wander into *The Bitch's* and so I took this as my opportunity to sneak out quickly, before I knew the inevitable happened. That tourist just looked *ripe* for asking directions. And I *hate*, all space smugglers *hate*, getting asked for directions.

So I sucked up the rest of my moiser, feeling that warm sting at the back of my throat, and then got to my feet.

I gave Drek and Lulub a slap each on the shoulder, wished them goodbye, then gave a less-fond goodbye glance to each of their waistcoats.

Fashion. I mean, really.

Funny habit of mine, but I said goodbye to the service droid too, gave him a cheery wave to go with it too. And perhaps that was my mistake. Maybe I made myself out to look approachable. *Friendly*. And, low and behold, when I stood ready to slink out the door, I heard that reedy, uneven voice in my right ear.

"Um, sir?"

I felt my stomach give a grumble, the way it does when I've taken a moiser down too fast. And I could feel a burp rumbling its way up my throat. But I held it in. For some reason I never feel all that comfortable burping planet-side. Maybe it's just my subconsciously stamped manners making a rare appearance.

I turned to look at the tourist, eyed him up and down again as if I hadn't seen him properly the first time, and then I snorted. In that intimidating way that smugglers tend to do. "What?"

The tourist broke out into a grin, shining me with a full head of teeth. It was a wonder that, the way he went about smiling at people in places like *The Bitch's*, that he hadn't lost them all. "I, uh, was interested in chartering a ship."

"Uh huh," I said, looking back over at Lulub and Drek, both of them now staring across at me, now also realising just what sort of a fix I was set in.

"Yeah, you see, I'm from Troblejon-8. I'm a—"

"*Tourist*," I said. "Yeah, I figured as much. You hardly fit in with the scenery, if you know what I mean?"

He chuckled too long and too hard, then tried to meet my eye.

I met his eye and gave his look back to him with a vengeance.

"Say," he said, "I'm interested in seeing something of Fritten, like to go see some of the planets while I'm about here. I'm all for paying the going rate, whatever that is."

At that point I just shrugged and took a step towards the door, already thinking about getting back to my beautiful, empty, quiet ship: the *Navaplastas*.

"Hey, wait!" the tourist said, then actually lurched forwards and grabbed a hold of my forearm.

Now, from a distance I pride myself on having what look to be pretty bulked-up forearms. At close quarters, though, I can appreciate that the effect's lost a little. If from a way away my forearms resemble tightly coiled steel cables, up close, and actually touching them, I guess it's more like fingering molten putty. And that was just what the tourist was finding out right now: finding out the fact that can just about sink any space smuggler worth his salt.

That he's not as tough as he looks.

As he stared at his fingers, gripping onto my forearm, as if he couldn't quite believe he'd just done what he'd just done, he got back to his quivering drivel. "Look, I've got money. Will you take money?"

I glanced across *The Bitch's*, right back to Lulub and Drek, both of them now fixing me with a slight sneer. I had half a mind to send this tourist packing, over in their direction, to go bother those fashion victims. But before I did my gut just took over. Told you I'm a smuggler, didn't I? And any smuggler's got something in his gut that takes over whenever money's mentioned.

"How much?" I said.

He told me.

I raised an eyebrow, glanced back across the bar, to the service droid, in the meantime trying to add up all the moisers I'd downed in the past few hours, and to calculate whether or not they'd messed up my brain.

I decided it was better to be safe than sorry. "Come again?" I said.

He told me again. Same figure.

I sat on the number a second or so, then sat on it a fraction of the following second. "All right, pal," I said. "You got yourself a deal."

2

HE WAS REASSURINGLY QUIET as we went through the terminal, and over to the bay where the *Nava* was parked. I turned round to him, lips only opening slightly, and said, "You mind looking the other way a moment?"

"Why's that?" the tourist said, clutching his suitcase, and frowning.

"Gotta do the security systems."

The tourist looked round my, sizeable, body to the front hatch of the security panel, and then he pouted. "Looks pretty serious to me. Certainly well beyond my abilities to crack it."

Now, if there's one way to get me on the right side, to get onto the road of being my friend—not that I have *any* friends—then you can go out and praise the *Nava*.

If, for some reason, you want to get me into bed, then go about praising the *Nava's* security systems.

I've spent some serious money on security over the years, a lot of *good* money. And I'd say it's just about the biggest source of pride for me in . . . well, in the entire galaxy, let's just leave it at that.

Still, despite this glowing compliment, I managed to keep up my smirk. "Yeah, but I still think you'd find those terminal windows just round there awfully interesting."

The tourist shrugged then turned away.

Guess I should've been glad that he didn't think to whack his camera out.

I got through with the security systems and then trudged in

through the door, and I listened to the slap of the tourist's sandals coming after me, then echoing about the metal walls of the corridor.

I drew in a great big breath as I arrived back on the bridge, and let out an enormous great sigh as I dropped back into the captain's chair, in all its battered, springy glory. And I just let that stench of my ingrained body odour seep into my nostrils, get back into my skin, and wash away that taste of moiser from my mouth.

Now, there's a bunch of laws about intoxication, going about driving a spaceship while you're half-cut. But, to be honest, I really couldn't give a crap. The other thing that the *Nava's* got in spades is laser cannons. Not that I've got myself a gunner yet.

Should probably look into that one of these days.

Still, the cannon looks pretty big—big enough that no backwater patrol from Hortenine-6 is gonna bother me. Also, I like to believe that I fly a whole lot better with some moiser in my stomach.

Guess we've all got beliefs, ain't we?

I slumped deeper into the captain's chair, feeling my body warmth collecting round me, and I reached out for the navigation panel, took a quick look over it. Guess it was for the best that I had a tourist on board, someone to pay passage, since, from the look of my navigational panel, and the communications, there weren't any jobs around for a good day or so's travel.

I heard that slap of sandal enter the bridge, and then that slightly whiny voice again. "Wow," the tourist said. "This really is a proper smuggler's ship, eh?"

"Suppose I'm supposed to take that as some kind of compliment?" I said, turning round in my chair, giving him my kindliest glare.

He held up his palms to me, like he was surrendering. "I'm just visiting," he said. "Just taking a look round, learning about how stuff works in the galaxy."

"Yeah, well, Tip Number One, and listen tight because this is a good one, whenever you're sitting in a spaceship that's about to jet outta port, you're almost always better served if you're seated and buckled in."

The tourist smiled faintly, then took up the seat at the laser cannons.

"Oh no," I said, flashing my eyes at him. "You can go over there." I pointed to seat on the other side of the bridge, the one I refer to as the kid's seat since it's far enough away from anything that matters. "Go on."

He snaffled hold of his suitcase and then beat his way over to the kid's seat. He sat down, and I watched him buckle himself in.

"Just one more thing," I said.

"What's that?"

"Gonna need to see some of that money."

3

JUST AS THE BOOSTERS FADED, I reached and felt for the throttle, brought it down several notches. And I felt that slight *hum* passing through my palms, jiggling my bones in that way I like . . . that I'm a little ashamed to say that I spend way to long enjoying on those long journeys of mine.

I glanced back to look at the tourist, and was glad to see that he was still in the kid's seat, glancing out through the port window just like a good little kiddie. He looked like he was pretty interested in all them stars going by. If it was true what he said about having come from Troblejon-8 then surely he'd seen enough stars to last him a lifetime . . . and then some.

Then again, I guess there're just some people that're weird about space like that. Never really seem to get over the awe of it.

The tourist caught me looking and wrestled with my gaze a while, before I reluctantly gave in. "So," I said, "where is it that you'd like me to take you?"

The tourist gave me a light smile, then a brief shrug. "Dunno, where do you suggest?"

I breathed in through my nostrils, again getting all that leathery smell, the upholstery of the captain's chair and the warmth of it all. And above everything else I was just glad to be back in the cockpit of the *Nava*, flying some place and getting paid for it. "That's up to you boss," I said. "To be honest, I ain't got much of an imagination when it comes to Fritten. Been round here pretty much my whole life, see? Can't really see it with fresh eyes, or whatever the hell it is they call it."

The tourist continued with his idiotic grin, then he glanced to the side, to my navigational screen. He looked over the list of planets, and our real-time location. He squinted at the map and, apparently at random, picked out a place, then said, "What about Poolkrantz-13?"

"Poolkrantz-13?" I said, trying to place it.

I thought back to my various jobs throughout Fritten and tried to get a handle on it. Nope. Nothing. Just as unsuspecting, or uninteresting place as there is in Fritten. I turned back to him. "What's so interesting about Poolkrantz-13?"

"A whole third of the place is a mega volcano, just wired to blow. Thought it might be an interesting thing for us to go see."

And there, right there. If I could pinpoint just where that tourist lost a whole bunch of points, it was in his insinuation that the *Nava* might get so much as a scratch on her . . . let alone splashed by an eruption from a volcano, the whole mega part of it was pretty irrelevant beyond that.

"Nah," I said. "No go."

The tourist cracked open his suitcase and flashed some more cash.

Guess we were going to Poolkrantz-13.

BACK AT HOME, growing up, we used to have a dog—dog called Garnie. Loved that mutt. Black all over, mixture of just about everything, and hearty stench, that I've made it my life's work to match for myself. If I can go to my grave stinking out the place as bad as Garnie did then I'll have made some mark on the universe.

Anyway, looking down at Poolkrantz-13 the first thing it reminded me of was when Garnie ate his way through a whole damn boxful of muffins and puked all over the front door mat.

Now, I'm all for being sensitive and all. I know that whenever I get onto the cusp of making some comment or other about some planet, I need to remind myself that someone lives down there—or most likely they do—and someone probably also proudly calls it home.

But, dammit, Poolkrantz-13 just looked like a great big pile of doggie sick.

And not healthy-dog doggie sick.

Just as I was turning up my nose, moving off to focus on my navigational screen rather than look out through the port hole at that sorry mess of a planet, I noticed the great yawning hole of a crater below me. The crater was just about the most attractive aspect of Poolkrantz-13. For one it was black. And you can't really go wrong with black. It's a classic. Maybe I'm not the most fashion conscious, but even an out-of-the-loop smuggler like me knows that.

Next thing I noted was that the damn crater was smoking

away, sending up a great wispy grey cloud. I looked back to the tourist, then said, "Last chance. Come to think of it maybe I ain't so blind when it comes to Fritten. Least I can think of a place that's a little better-looking than *this*."

The tourist just peered out through the porthole, smiling gently, sitting in the kid's seat and keeping his hands to himself.

I gave a little sigh and then descended through the atmosphere, setting our coordinates for the Poolkrantz-13 terminal.

5

W E'D ONLY JUST about set down in the terminal, when I caught the tourist shucking off his straps, and leaping up out of the kid's seat. I frowned at him, but he paid me no attention. He just went scarpering off along the corridor. Only when he reached the well-secured door to the *Nava*, did he have to call after me. "Um, sir? Would you mind?"

I glanced back at the kid's seat, saw that his suitcase was still stuffed beneath it. And, more importantly, all that lovely money stuffed inside it, and so I gave a little shrug and undid the locks on the door.

From the comfort of the captain's chair, I watched him skitter out from the under belly of the *Nava*, totter across the terminal dock, and then disappear into the terminal building.

There's one thing that marks a decent smuggler above your everyday, garden-variety one. And that's knowing when there's a chance to catch a nap.

That was my chance.

6

ONE THING THAT RILES ME up something rotten, aside from people trashing my ship, or worse: the security systems, is getting woken up. Over the time I've been a smuggler—most of my life—I've always been able to catch a nap while floating out in open space. No real chance of getting bothered out there, I can tell you. Napping in terminals is different, though. There's always the chance of some busybody customs officer or some inspector of whatever sort wanting to drop in on you, 'Just to check up on things.'

In this case, though, what woke me up wasn't any employee or hanger-on from the terminal, but my . . . well, I suppose I could call him my client.

He woke me up banging his fists against the door to the *Nava*. And, let me tell you, I was of half a mind to slip on over to the laser cannon and give him a dozen or so of the best. Maybe it was my groggy sleepiness that saved him, or perhaps the promise of that suitcase and it's mountains of cash, but I disengaged the locks and let him inside.

Thinking about it now, I already *had* the cash right there with me. Never was top of my class or nothin' . . .

The slap of those sandals sounded along the corridor, and I noticed that each step was also accompanied by a slight *grunt*, as if the tourist was carrying some heavy object or other. I turned in my seat to see him entering the bridge with, what I can only describe as, a big-ass rock in his hands.

I glared at him, feeling my eyelids pound on my forehead. "What in hell's name is that you've got there?"

The tourist dropped the rock on the floor, and it clanged against it, the sound echoing off into the ship like a rock tossed into a tin can . . . but a much bigger scale, of course. He fell back into the kid's seat and I saw the sweat shining on his face. "Rock," he said, in between long, hard breaths.

"Yeah," I said. "Not sure quite what you've heard about smugglers but we tend to be at least sharp enough to know a rock when we see one. Question is, what the hell's it doing on my ship?"

The tourist gulped down more air. "This . . . is . . . what . . . I . . . . came . . . for."

"Really? Had not guessed *that*."

The tourist kept taking in air, folded over himself, and then seemed to get a grip on the basics of breathing once more. He jerked his thumb back over his shoulder, to indicate the way down the corridor, back to the door of the *Nava*. "They're coming after us. We'd better get a move on."

And just then I glanced out through the window and—what do you know?—I saw ten or so officers all fully armed and emerging from the terminal building. I did a quick calculation in my brain, working out just how much I'd been paid, and how much I would be paid following a successful escape from Poolkrantz-13, then weighed that against 'doing the right thing' and handing this thieving bastard over to the authorities.

Thinking done, I hit the throttle, felt the blasters take hold and get us floating a couple metres up in the air.

I looked over those officers, all forming up now, under the

instruction of their superior, all of them packing a blaster rifle. I glanced back at the tourist. "You can scoot on over to the laser cannon seat now, all right?"

The tourist did as I told him, buckled up there, and then I hammered off the brakes and the *Nava* soared right up into space.

7

W E'D BEEN rolling about five minutes out of Poolkrantz-13, when I turned back to the tourist and said, "Just where do you get off doing that, huh? Didn't want to tell me just what it was that you wanted from Poolkrantz-13?"

The tourist blushed a touch, then looked back to the rock, which had somehow stayed secured during take-off, and was still very much stowed beneath the kid's seat.

"Go on, then," I said, glancing at the navigational screen. "Tell me what's going on. I know I'm not gonna like it, but tell me anyhow."

The tourist blinked a couple of times, then put on the most sheepish of sheepish grins. "You're right," he said. "I'm not much of a tourist, not really. Back on Poolkrantz-13 I work for the largest energy supplier, Horclux Energy, and they sent me out here to snaffle this here rock and bring it back to them." He nodded to the rock beneath the kid's seat. "It's basically like a great big natural battery."

My smuggler brain just about caught up with that brief breeze of science, and I said, "You mean kinda like a baked potato?"

"Same principle," the tourist said, then sighed a little. "In any case, it's really gonna save our bacon back on Poolkrantz. We've been struggling, see, because the planet Obliteron's been slashing the price of hench for just about as long as they've been supplying it, and so Horclux has been having to find new ways, new processes, to stay afloat. And since so much of our economy's wrapped up with energy, that so many of our livelihoods depend on it, then it's really become imperative that I get this rock here back there."

"Uh huh, I'd like to say that I understood a fraction of what you just said, but my mumma always taught me not to tell lies. Come to think of it she also told me never to become a space bum. I guess mothers always know best, huh?"

The tourist just smiled on, and continued as if I hadn't said anything at all. "So thanks so much for bringing me out here all this way," he said.

"I'd say it's my pleasure, but the two of us know that's not the real reason. I'm a mercenary, pure and simple. If the money's right, I'll do it. Pretty much that's always been my motto, in any case." I glanced to the navigational screens, checking out our current location, and if there was anyone following us. Seeing that there wasn't, I glanced back at him. "Where to now, chief?"

He smiled then said, "Back to Hortenine-6, I can catch a ship out of there, back to Poolkrantz."

"Your wish is my command."

8

WE ROLLED BACK into the dock at Hortenine-6, and the tourist crossed my palm with silver for my troubles. All said it turned out pretty nicely. I got a great big payday, and the tourist got off with his rock, or whatever the hell it was, to take back to his people on his planet.

I never did think to ask his name, but that's probably just my heartless side coming out. I've always thought that it doesn't pay to get close to people, and often just the reverse is true. Thing is that sentiment can often leave you out of pocket. And, as the long-living space smuggler knows, you can't survive long out on your own if you've got no money to pump your ship full of fuel.

I slouched back into *The Bitch's* to find both Drek or Lulub still there. They looked a little drunker, and the droid looked a little wearier—that's right, life on Hortenine even gets to the droids. Still, I didn't want to be impolite so I ordered a moiser, pulled up a stool, and then slapped myself down next to those two reprobates.

Oh sure, they pulled my leg this way and that about having to go off and take the tourist on his little trip about Fritten, but when they asked about the money I got all vague and they saw right through me. If there's one thing that a smuggler'll never talk about it's whatever he got paid for his latest job. Still, you get pretty good, pretty quick, at reading other smugglers, so much so that you can easily read between the lines.

And Drek and Lulub could read between the lines.

So, imagine my delight, when, into my fifth moiser, the door of

42

The Bitch's went *creak-creak* and another likely-looking gentleman poked on in. He had a suitcase too, just like the tourist, and I had a little chuckle to myself as I watched Drek and Lulub elbow each other to get themselves across the bar, and over to him.

As for me, I just finished up that moiser, gave the service droid a friendly tap on the shoulder, then snuck on out, headed back to the terminal, and back to the *Navaplastas*. Never has been my bag to pick up work in a bar since then. Picking up work in a bar can get you into a whole lot of trouble.

Buyers' market and all that.

As I sat there at the controls of the *Nava*, I sat back and wondered just what sort of shape Drek or Lulub would be in next time I'd see them down *The Bitch's*. I wondered if they'd be in any shape at all, because the history of space smuggling's thick with the stories of the smugglers that picked up work in a bar and never did rear their heads again. Either they got the Big Payoff, or they just got themselves drowned somehow.

In my case, though, I know that the Big Payoff'll never come, that I'll spend the rest of my life bumbling about the galaxy from job to job, never really finding direction, having a bunch of great adventures.

And, for me, that's just fine.

BAND OF LIARS

1

RULE ONE of the *Space Smuggler Handbook* might be: *Never Pick Up Work In Bars* but a fairly close second would certainly be: *Never Get Yourself On The Wrong End Of The Interstellar Hires Bay*. And the wrong end for a smuggler like me means to be the one forking out for the 'privilege' of using some reprobate pilot's ship.

That said, the worst part about trying to charter a ship out of the Interstellar Hires Bay is the band of liars hanging about the place. The po-faced, sell-their-grandmother, shameless, money-grabbing, hard-bargaining *liars*.

I mean *you* try doing some business with these types who'd just as soon as dump you five minutes out of atmosphere as transport you to your intended destination.

And all because they decided they didn't like your face.

But needs must.

Sometimes there's no way around Interstellar Hires, especially when your ship is in for repairs.

Believe me, if the *Navaplastas* was in any sort of shape for the job I decided to take on then I would never—*in a million years*—have resorted to running the gauntlet in Interstellar Hires.

I suppose the follow-up question to that would be to ask why I took on the job at all if I didn't have my noble spaceship all juiced up and ready to go . . . and the short answer to that would be:

Credits.

And the long answer?

Lots of credits.

As Arkle Wright—smuggler of universe-wide renown . . . I know how that sounds, but it's the truth—I've ended up with a certain reputation . . . well, hang about, 'reputation' probably makes it sound far more formal than it really is . . . why not just settle on the understanding that a certain *odour* follows me around. And certain people have learned to associate that *odour* with a certain degree of success. Yeah, either that or people see my cute, pudgy little face and think I'll do just about anything. Never underestimate the Look of Desperation.

And so I found myself treading on along the polished-up tiles of Interstellar Hires, on Uranax-1.

Don't go looking through your star charts for a Uranax-2 or -3, or whatever else, because you won't find it . . . Uranax is one of those *unique* systems that feels it needs to keep up with the Joneses in such matters as numbering. Systems with only a single planet have to be the one sure-fire criteria for identifying accompanying nutso locals . . . something which comes in handy for a space smuggler; because if there's one thing I've learned down the years, it's that you need to *know* the people you're dealing with. It's not only the best way to make money, it's the best way to prevent getting your belly—and other vital appendages—sliced open.

That said, Uranax-1 hadn't been at all bad of a slog.

Oh, there'd been the usual unpleasantness with the food and the water, the stomach cramps, all of that backwater-planet stuff. But, abdominal issues aside, I'd had no room for complaint . . . other than the fact that some irritating atmospheric dust had done for a good portion of the *Nava's* electrical components.

On that particular job, I'd been enlisted by word-of-mouth to deliver a quite fetching—*if frighteningly dull*—golden pocket watch. And one which I'd taken to hanging from the pocket of my thermal waistcoat by its golden chain. In some ways it made me feel like a gentleman.

And, in some others, a pimp . . .

Way I saw it, one or the other of those images would serve me well when it came to shielding myself from the more manic of the looney contingent.

How wrong I was.

Whenever possible, I go out of my way to follow advice—especially when it's my own—as I was doing on that particular job. What your mamma said was right. You can tell a lot about a person from a first impression.

Like *everything*.

If a certain individual has a strand of drool dangling down from the corner of their mouth—a vacant look in their eyes—then that's probably someone you wouldn't much like to be entrusted to the controls when the proximity alarms are shrieking and evasive action cries out to be taken.

Another pet hate of mine, and one which I saw often enough at the Interstellar Hires on Uranax, is the posers. You know the type. The ones who're *dressed to kill*—usually outfitted in some *too-tight* leather cat suit with a blaster slipped into their thigh holster . . . arms crossed over their chest. Now, understand me, it's not because I believe these people exude false confidence at all —*oh, no*—it's been the sum of my experience that those who make a show of being competent generally very much *are* so . . . in other words, they have terrific reasons for looking that way; veterans of many a shoot-out, many a dog-fight, many a bar-brawl . . . and, yeah, that's not really what you're looking for when, as a smuggler, all you really want to do is drop off some product and make some credits.

I strode on by *those* types.

Finally, I got almost to the end of the Interstellar Hires Bay and knew that if I didn't pick out one of the remaining pilots then I'd have to double back and make the best of a bad bunch—it was out of the question that I was going to give up on this job paying cold, hard credits.

I prepared myself for the dawning disappointment—not too daunting seeing as I've dealt with disappointment, in one form or another, every single day of my life.

Disappointment I can handle.

It's *hope* that kills.

Then I caught sight of the penultimate pilot at Interstellar Hires.

She stood between a pair of those cat-suited, confidence jobs and was conspicuous by contrast. Silver-grey hair. Leathery, tightly wrinkled skin. Hands softened by a pair of fingerless gloves . . . the type which I'm quite partial to wearing myself.

I approached her.

"Well, hello there," I said, feeling a slight warmth clinging to my jubbly stomach.

For some reason, I felt a familiar spark in my chest.

Something which made my heart thump.

Did I recognise her?

The woman turned to me and narrowed her eyes. She cocked her head to one side. "Arkle? Is that you?"

Despite myself, I realised I was blushing.

The blood rising in my cheeks.

50

Say what you will about smugglers, in a way we're like film stars, we never quite tire of being recognised—of having our work *validated* in the real world.

"Yes, ma'am," I replied with a nod. "Arkle Wright, at your service"—I switched tact right at that point realising I was the one doing the soliciting of services today—"I mean, pleased to meet you."

"Don't you recognise me?"

I peered closer; took in her silver hair; her leathery wrinkles. "I can't rightly say that I do."

The old woman crushed her lips together in a pout.

I'd apparently done something unforgiveable to stoke her ire.

. . . As I said, you've gotta take care in these backwater places like Uranax-1.

"You don't recognise your own *grandmother*?"

2

W E SPED AWAY from Uranax-1, leaving that tight ball of greenish, blue silver they call a planet behind. We were travelling in my grandmother's ship.

Now, let me get one thing straight, since I've been bombing about the universe on a wing and a prayer I've run into just about every single scam going. And the old, *I'm-your-grandmother* or *I'm-your-long-lost-aunt-slash-cousin-slash-half-brother* has been run so many times that the well is truly dry.

I'd like to say that I haven't learned that particular lesson through personal experience, but that'd make me just as bad as that band of liars that make up the Interstellar Hires Bay of just about any terminal in the universe you care to mention. The point is, I knew this wasn't my grandmother. All it would take for her to pull a fast one on me was to find out my name and appearance— perhaps learn of my unfortunate predicament with the *Nava*—and play on my own sense of nostalgia.

But I never knew my grandmother.

Never knew much about my family, really.

And, if I'd been in the mood for being fooled at all, then surely the fact that my own grandmother had nothing of the Arkle-4 accent about her would've set alarm bells ringing. Still, I decided that I had the upper-hand; let the old lady believe whatever she *wanted* to believe.

I turned to examine the cockpit of the ship again.

A seriously nice piece of work.

Chrome fixtures.

Meaty-looking throttle.

And the seats . . . wow, I have to tell you, it got me thinking that I should look into having the seats of the *Nava* reupholstered while she was in for repairs. If I'd had the credits to spend on something so lavish as that then I certainly would've done so.

The pilot—*my grandmother*—slipped me a sidelong glance. "What's that you've got there?"

I glanced about, having forgotten the golden pocket watch I was supposed to be transporting to the next planet over. "Oh, this," I said, immediately putting up my guard—telling myself that I couldn't afford to give this *woman* a chance to fool me . . . for all I knew this pocket watch of mine might be worth a fortune. Often, when somebody wanted to get something of great value through a bit of space, they'd get hold of some fleabag freelancer to do it for them . . . an understated touch, or so I'm told.

The woman rested one hand on the joystick—the ship now on autopilot; flying itself—and then reached out for the pocket watch. "May I see, dear?"

I held back for a long moment before telling myself that I had to tread carefully. This wasn't *my* ship, of course, and the woman— *my 'grandmother'*—would be well within her rights as captain to blast me clean out through the airlock. And that particular day I wasn't in the mood for a cooling-off. "Sure," I said, finally, and worked to undo the chain from where I'd fastened it to my thermals. I handed it over to her.

She took it from me. She held it up to the cockpit light, squinting slightly.

Feeling as if I should make conversation, and unable to hold back my snark any longer, I said, "Do you need me to find your glasses, *Grandma?*"

She slipped me a cold glance, no doubt testing the waters to see if I'd discovered her imitation games. But, apparently deciding I hadn't, she smiled back pleasantly. "No, dear, thank you—I have perfectly augmented vision . . . I was merely taking a look at the structural makeup of the gold."

And, with that, apparently done 'looking at the structural makeup of the gold' she neatly snapped the pocket watch in two, revealing the clock face within.

Now, if there was ever such a thing as a Smugglers' Union and —*Godforbid*—some kind of set of ethics, I can well imagine that discretion of the client would feature quite highly as a value in a trustworthy smuggler. However, no union—and certainly no *ethics* —exist for space smugglers.

That said, I hadn't actually taken the time to have a gander at the pocket watch yet . . . most likely due to my worry for the *Nava.* The best way I can think to describe it is like when a close member of family is undergoing surgery. When your *spouse* is undergoing surgery.

I took a peek over 'Grandma's' shoulder and saw that the clock face of the pocket watch was Really Quite Pleasant Indeed . . . which was to say it had those same quaint analogue hands, the same peeling, yellowing backdrop, the same Roman numerals in place of *ordinary* numbers . . . I just about forgot the appearance of the pocket watch as soon as I processed it through my brain.

"Shame," 'Grandma' said, with a sigh, handing the pocket watch back to me.

"Why's that?"

'Grandma' shrugged then turned back to the controls of the ship. "It's a piece of junk—*worthless.*"

I did my best to suppress a smile as I clipped the pocket watch back onto my thermals, recognising this as yet another of those very old confidence tricks.

Some people in this universe really do believe I was born yesterday.

As we rocked on to the destination, 'Grandma' spoke to me once again, in an off-hand sort of a way. "You don't believe me, Arkle, do you?"

"Believe what?"

"That I'm your grandmother."

I waited out a beat, then decided I needed to respond. "No," I said, firmly, already convinced that I'd made a mistake, that I was going to be needing the space blaster holstered to my thigh before too long. I suppose it was a mercy she didn't have a space blaster of her own.

Not strapped to her thigh, out in plain sight, anyway.

"Can I show you something?" she said, out of nowhere, rising up out of her chair.

I watched her head towards the back of the cockpit.

And I knew that if I was going to seize control of the ship, take my destiny in my own two hands, then I better well do it right now.

I hesitated.

"Come on," she said. "I promise I won't bite."

SOME MEN are suckers for alcohol.

Others for space blasters.

More still for their ships.

I'm all those and more.

And why not call me a sucker for motherly figures while you're about it?

Which probably makes *grandmotherly* figures something like a lethal dose.

As I followed in 'Grandma's' footsteps, I couldn't help but notice all the neat little touches within her ship. How she had several framed cross-stitches of Earthlike landscapes; how she had a whole system of planets rendered into knitted balls of synthetic wool; and, like just about any old person I'd ever met, she had her fair share of trinkets—things which twizzled and sparkled— dangling away at the end of silver or gold chains.

I made a point of grabbing for my pocket watch. I wondered if, given that she clearly *valued* these things which hung from her walls—and them *clearly* being junk—then might it not mean that she'd been exactly one-hundred-per-cent incorrect when placing a valuation on the pocket watch?

Perhaps.

I had to watch her close.

Old ladies can be wily.

Especially around me.

They *smell* the fear.

However, 'Grandma' didn't venture over to one of the aforementioned trinkets and dish it out to me as some kind of lost treasure; instead she headed on over to a large, wooden box. I was fairly certain that it was a kind of rosewood—*ersatz rendering most likely*—and, strangely given the surroundings, it made the ship seem a little more cosy.

From within the box, she withdrew a scroll.

With a practised flick of the wrist, she snapped it open to reveal the clear screen within.

Almost like a pair of human eyelashes fluttering at first light, the screen of the scroll blinked twice and then shone its light-blue, start-up glow over the corridor.

She looked to me.

Smiled.

"I think this will prove it to you once and for all."

I had to admit that this show of confidence—if that was what it could be called—was beginning to actually have a profound effect on me.

As I stood there, watching on, she controlled the scroll with her mind.

I observed as she brought up the Browse screen, showing off a whole myriad of photographs; all of them stylised with a sort of film ribbon.

Even then, I felt myself begin to melt inside, because I knew just what I was looking at.

Despite the images still being rendered in miniature, I could identify the faces.

My mother.

My father.

My brother.

Myself.

And, as 'Grandma' brought the reel to a standstill, I saw that there was another among them . . . a woman with silver hair.

'Grandma' maximised the current image.

It filled the entirety of the scroll.

Then held it up as if I couldn't already see it well enough from how she held it in her hands.

"See?" she said.

Almost right away, I felt the tears prickle at the corners of my eyes.

Almost as quick, I blinked them away, and then coughed to myself as if it'd do a good job of covering up the crude reaction.

Finally, when I got myself back together, I turned my attention to the image.

There, sure enough, I saw myself—as a child; no older than three or four—with my mother, my brother—*still a baby*—and my 'Grandma' with her silver hair, appearing just as she did before my eyes right now. I stared at the image for another few seconds before glancing up at her.

There was no need to say anything, she seemed to be able to read my current state of mind.

And, since we were blood relatives, I decided that was no out-of-reach feat.

Finally, I managed to get something out. "Thank you," I said. "Thank you for showing me."

With a doleful nod, Grandma—no need for the quotation marks now—snapped the scroll shut and replaced it in the rose-wood box. When she turned to face me, she glanced down absentmindedly at the pocket watch hanging from my thermals. "I know this brings up a lot of questions—a lot of *emotions*."

Although I tried not to give anything away, I knew that by this stage there was nothing left *to* give away . . . and, in any case, what would be the point in holding back?

"Why didn't you stay? Why didn't you stay on Arkle-4?"

She shook her head then snorted a laugh.

I could see that a few tears clung to her eyes.

"The same reason as *you*."

I pressed my lips together, supposing that I was beginning to better see the family resemblance. "Why didn't you ever come to visit?"

"Some years back me and Big Jo had a misunderstanding. To say I'm persona non grata in Arkle-4 is like saying smuggling is a noble and upstanding profession."

I turned my mind to Big Jo—the mobster who runs things back on Arkle-4 . . . the man who, for want of a better description, *terrorises* the planet . . . and who had continued to do so for all I knew; because, I, just like my Grandma, hadn't been back.

As if this fact drifted down over the two of us, a silence snuck up on our conversation.

Grandma nodded to the pocket watch still hanging at my thermals. "We should be getting on. We'll be entering orbit soon." And, with that, she paced past me, headed for the cockpit.

I stood about like some kind of dunce for another few moments before following.

4

I HAVE TO ADMIT, for the first time since the *Nava* got dinged-up, I was glad not to be the one doing the flying. I stared down through the view screens to the ominous, glowing-coal red planet below. If a little bit of dust in the atmosphere had done so much damage to the *Nava* then there'd be no telling just how much damage *lava* would do to a spaceship.

But apparently this was the destination:

Volcanus-4.

Where I was meant to drop off the pocket watch.

Grandma seemed to be having the same reservations. "You're sure this is the place?"

"Uh-huh."

"Legally, I've gotta inform you about the damage liability waiver you signed before stepping on this ship; and, on board my baby, the rule has always been, *Client pays damage.*"

"Huh?" I said, turning in my chair to look at her.

I wasn't all that surprised about the contents of what she'd said —to be honest, most of us smugglers live by the same rules . . . although that bullshit about a 'damage liability waiver' was just that. I was more surprised to think that she'd said anything at all.

Why say anything at all?

"Is that clear?" she said, fiddling about with the joystick, bringing us down into the atmosphere.

"You want to see the credits, or something?"

I took in her smile side-on; in profile. "Nah, family is what it is." She glanced to me for a second, and I was certain that I saw genuine affection.

True to her word, Grandma brought us down through the rocky atmosphere; through what I would've defined for myself as being something approaching a 'firestorm' . . . Grandma, though, seemed unaffected by the situation—totally cool and calm.

How I'd like to imagine *myself* acting in similar circumstances.

The terminal was up on a mountain top; one of the few spots on this planet which didn't seem to contain a volcano. It had been extended with a whole bunch of platforms jutting out at all angles. From the look of the ships parked up—and more likely the red-coloured dust which coloured them—I could tell that this wasn't much more than the backwater I'd already pinned it to be.

As Grandma brought her ship down, I caught sight of the Fritten System flag flapping about in the blazing hot air; and I could see that it'd got all singed about the edges.

Once the airlock blasted on open, and the ventilation shifted from cabin to atmosphere, I caught a heady stench of sulphur . . . or—to put it a little more bluntly—*rotten eggs*.

The air, too, was stiflingly hot.

But it seemed to affect me more than Grandma given my 'cuddly' frame.

It was when we got through terminal control, past the sleeping, septuagenarian official cushioning his head with folded arms on his desk, that I started to get antsy.

I'd been told to bring the pocket watch here, to the terminal on this Godforsaken planet.

I'd then been given the instruction that 'someone' would find *me*.

I supposed that whoever was in charge of this switch, or whatever it was that was going on, had an image of me somewhere to compare with the real-live version that'd just strutted on into the terminal. Somehow I couldn't quite get myself to believe they'd have any sort of DNA scanner; but, then again, I've been wrong about these things before . . .

What'd most dragged me in about this job—what'd got me to leave the planet where my dear *Nava* was getting patched up— was the promise that I'd be greeted on arrival with the full payment of the job . . . there'd be none of that scratching about searching for the low-life that'd given me the job in the first place so that they would cough up the other half of the payment. For a space smuggler, payment is the majority of the battle. The rest is all *gravy* in comparison.

I looked from one side of the terminal to the other, the pocket watch still hanging from the waistcoat of my thermals. Grandma was still standing beside me, her arms crossed, waiting for me to get my credits so that she might get hers.

Finally, I spotted some shifty-looking soul.

Someone in a denim jacket.

Collar popped.

Wide-brimmed hat drawn low.

I wrinkled my brow as they approached.

Captain Obvious, or what?

As Captain Obvious got closer still, hands still stuffed in their pockets, I unlatched the watch from where it hung off me. And I held it in my palm, kind of glad to be getting shot of it.

Captain Obvious arrived before me, and then, in a strained voice, said, "You got it?"

"Uh-huh," I replied, thrusting the pocket watch at them.

Captain Obvious took it off me.

If they looked over the pocket watch a single second, then I missed it.

Captain Obvious shifted off.

Away from me.

I didn't miss a trick.

I reached out and grabbed hold of their jacket sleeve. "Hey! You ain't got the credits, have you?"

Captain Obvious turned around.

For a second, I thought I might've seen some eyes . . . but then there was only shadow.

"Later," Captain Obvious said. "They'll be along in a few minutes."

I kept up my hold. "Uh-uh. That's not gonna happen."

Captain Obvious kept up their resistance, but at no point attempted to squirm free of my grip. I'd made sure that I'd put my blaster on show as Captain Obvious had approached, on the theory that it would hopefully put paid to any funny business. I guess I needed to cut the subtlety.

I reached down for my holster.

For my space blaster.

Nothing.

"Shit!" I inadvertently shouted.

I spun around, still holding Captain Obvious firmly, and caught sight of Grandma.

She stood with her legs a perfect shoulders-width apart and held my blaster pointed at the two of us. "Give him the credits," she said.

I kept hold of Captain Obvious, hoping to drive some sense into them.

I guessed quite a few qualities had passed down through the genes.

That all-important gene which helps you to make sure that everybody along the chain gets their cash so that you get your own.

Captain Obvious remained still.

Then I felt them begin to chuckle.

The vibration of it passing all the way along my arm.

"What's so funny?" I asked, trying to sound as obstinate as possible.

Captain Obvious just laughed more and more.

I attempted to get a glance at their face, but no dice.

That hat and upturned collar were keeping their identity concealed.

I kept a tighter hold.

Tugged Captain Obvious towards me.

"You listen here, and you listen good. You hand over those credits, and you hand them over this second, got it?"

Captain Obvious just kept laughing.

Shaking their head now.

I was about to lose my mind.

It was probably a good thing I didn't have my space blaster.

I would've hated to be held accountable for my actions.

A flash of light derailed my train of thought.

Then pain ripped through my right forearm.

"*Argh!*" I let out, releasing Captain Obvious as I did so.

I dropped to the ground, onto my knees.

Captain Obvious trod back a couple of steps before breaking into a run.

I turned my attention upwards, to the terminal, wondering why in all hell Grandma had decided to shoot me . . . or perhaps her eyes simply weren't as good as she thought they were.

However, that thought ended just as quickly as it had begun, because, lying on my back now, cradling my afflicted right arm to my chest, I watched on as she brought Captain Obvious down with a pair of perfectly aimed blaster shots.

One in the back of each knee.

Captain Obvious fell with a scream to rival my own.

I heard the distant sound of metal on tile as the pocket watch slipped through their grasp.

My eyes filled with tears.

My heart beat its way further and further up my throat.

When I looked back to Grandma, I saw she'd taken up a different posture—that she was down on one knee, propping up the blaster with her other arm and taking aim at some target above our heads.

I turned my attention upwards.

Saw the barrel of a blaster rifle.

Blasts spewing forth from it.

With another few well-aimed shots, Grandma brought the shooting to a stop.

I glanced back to see that a satisfied coil of smoke was rising from the barrel of *my* space blaster.

Grandma unfurled herself from the crouched position she'd taken up to bring Captain Obvious and the shooter down. As she approached me, she wore a satisfied smirk. One of those smirks which—if it'd been anyone else other than, (one) a woman, or (two), my own grandmother—I'd have taken great pleasure in bulldozing.

5

GRANDMA REACHED OUT a supporting hand. "You okay?"

Her voice sounded slightly different.

Something about it I couldn't put my finger on.

A more nasal tone?

I was loath to relinquish my good hand from its current duty in cradling my shot-up one, but decided that now was not the time to come across as a *sissy* boy . . . I hadn't got paid yet, after all.

Once back on my feet, Grandma leaned over my injured arm; frowned at it, and then reached into her flight suit. From one of the zip-up pockets, she produced a spray can. "Bite your lip," she said, her voice still sounding a little funny.

I didn't have time to do as she instructed.

Thankfully, though, the high-pitched sound of the spray leaving the nozzle of the can dampened the worst of my groan.

She withdrew the can, and I watched on as the flesh about the blaster wound healed; the skin knitting into itself like a possessed ball of yarn. Within about a minute, the skin was back to normal.

I blinked back the remaining pain—now only a vague heat—and then glanced back at her, a smile smeared across my lips. "Get that through Army Surplus?"

"Something like that," she said, replacing the can in the pocket she had retrieved it from.

There was still something in the air that I hadn't quite been able to put my finger on.

But I was certain there *was* something.

Grandma busied herself, stalking over to Captain Obvious. She crouched down, picked up the pocket watch, glanced it over another time and then tossed it to one side.

As she crouched there, I noted how her hair seemed to be . . . *changing*.

Whereas before it'd been that silvery-grey; now it had taken on a darker shade . . . yes, it was slowly tinting itself a brunette colour.

I wondered how much tech like that cost.

But, at that moment in time, it seemed somewhat beside the point.

The more pertinent question was *why* it was happening right then.

With a shake of her head, Grandma got to her feet. She kicked at the pocket watch, sending it skittering across the terminal floor. Her back still turned towards me, she said, "Worthless piece of junk."

"Huh?" I said, and then remembered the pocket watch. "Oh, it is?"

Grandma turned back to me. "Planted by us."

I felt the blood rushing to my head. " 'Us' ?"

Grandma nodded, and I saw that what had once been leathery skin had become far more toned—more *youthful*. "Yep," she said, absentmindedly handing me back my blaster.

I took it from her, stashing it back in my thigh holster.

'Grandma'—there are those quotation marks again—turned her attention up to the shooter who'd been trying to fry us with the rifle from above. She squinted, doing the same thing she'd done back in the cockpit when I'd made that crack about her eyesight. A smile tugged at the corner of her lips. She reached up to her ear and pressed her finger inside. "Got him," she said, seeming to speak to someone else on the other end of a communicator.

As I traced 'Grandma' I noticed how her step became all the more spry. Her back again turned to me, she rolled her shoulders as if loosening built-up tension, while she spoke to the person on the other end of the communicator.

I just stood about like a dummy for another few minutes.

While she finished the call.

When she turned back to me, the expression on her—now-youthful; and completely *unrecognisable* face—seemed to express the idea that she had genuinely forgotten I was there at all. "Oh," she said, and then narrowed one eye. "Arkle?"

I scratched at the new skin on my shot-up arm. "Uh-huh."

"Thanks for your help—it was most valuable to have you on board for this operation."

" 'Operation' ?"

'Grandma' busied herself with another one of her pockets; before finally reaching up to her eye, apparently communicating again with whoever was on the other end. When she got off the line this time, she began to stride towards the dock.

The shock was still resounding through my skull; both at what had transpired, and that my 'Grandma' had disintegrated before my very eyes and been replaced by this youthful *girl*.

"Hey!" I called out, surprised at the strength in my voice.

'Grandma' wheeled around. At first, she wore a bemused expression, which quickly transitioned to a false-looking smile. "Yes?"

"What just happened?"

'Grandma' reached up for her inner-ear communicator again.

69

I cut her off. "Hey!"

She brought her hand back as if something within her ear might've snapped at her fingers.

"What's going on?!"

'Grandma' smiled back at me again—that same *false* smile—and then she took a couple of steps towards me. "A sting. You've been a great help, Arkle."

"I have?"

"Yes," she went on, all her attention—at least for the time being—focussed on me. "We wanted to get to the shooter"—she pointed up vaguely to where the shooter lay dead—"and to do so, we got our hands on that pocket watch . . . some trinket which once belonged to his mother; and which he was keen to get back." She shook her head. "He's always been reluctant to come out in the open so it was a real coup to trap him like this." Her expression became all at once more solemn. "You have no idea how many of our agents he's killed."

Something in my brain crackled away.

I felt as if I was spinning around impossibly fast on the spot.

Somehow, though, I managed to get out the important question:

"Who is *us*?"

'Grandma' slapped her forehead in a way which belied the age she'd previously been trying to convey. "Oh, that's right—I didn't say."

"No, you didn't."

She cracked a nervous smile. "FSA—Fritten System Authorities . . . that's all I can tell you, I'm afraid . . ." She trod back towards me, held out her hand for me to shake.

Still bemused, I accepted it.

"Thank you, Arkle. You've been most helpful."

With that, she tried to get away again.

"Wait!" I called out.

She turned once more.

I shook my head. "My grandmother . . . are you . . . who was . .
."

"Listen, when the opportunity presented itself we had to come up with something. The idea was to have you lead us right to the shooter—so we could take care of him . . . which I did . . ."

"But"—I shook my head—"I still don't . . ."

Again, she slapped herself on the forehead. "Oh, you mean"—she flapped her hands to indicate her, now quite spritely, body —"yes, well, it wasn't that difficult. We only had to get hold of some of your personal images. Manipulate them . . ."

My chest tightened. "Then, my real grandmother?"

She winced. "No idea, I'm afraid. At least *I* don't know . . . I'm only a grunt assassin." Here she made a childish gun-shooting motion with her fingers. "Will that be all?" she asked, a slight note of exasperation in her voice now.

"The bodies?"

"Ah, yes." She scowled then rubbed her temple. "No, we're supposed to leave them here—to send a message."

"I see."

She stepped away.

And I followed.

Once we'd got a few steps, she turned.

Gave me a pleasant smile.

"Where're you off to?"

"Uh, I was hoping I could hitch a lift with you."

She beamed back at me. "Sorry, I won't be able to do that." She threw up her hands. "Forms, protocols, all that . . . since the operation's over now I can't go ferrying people about places—I might be needed."

"You're leaving me here?" I said.

She reached up and tapped her inner ear. Then tilted her head and smiled. "I've got word that an FSA-chartered ship should be along in the next day or so."

"Oh, okay," I replied, pleasantly surprised.

"Yes," she went on. "The only thing is that day here—on this planet—lasts six weeks."

" 'Six weeks' !"

"I'm sure it'll *fly* by," she said, with a quick grin, and hurried onwards.

I kept up on her heels. "What am I going to do in all that time?"

She shrugged. "See the sights."

I looked out through the terminal window, to the landscape covered with volcanoes. To the sooty ash which constantly rose up into the sky, blackening out any prospect of natural light.

She continued on her way as if this was an effective argument. "You'll be adequately recompensed for your role in the operation."

"How much?"

She told me.

That was just about the only acceptable part of the conversation.

I knew that there was more to say—more avenues I could explore to try and convince her to take me back with her to

Uranax-1—but I was sick of arguing; and, I suppose, a little dazzled by the money which was on offer.

I stood up at the terminal window, watching on as 'Grandma's' ship rose into the atmosphere and then blasted on out into space.

With all the credits 'Grandma' had in the pipeline for me, I could pimp out the *Navaplastas* any which way I wanted.

Perhaps *some* good had come out of this band of liars after all .

. .

LUBBARDLY COWARDS

1

NOT MUCH ELSE gets my goat more than people obsessed with animals. Oh sure, they're cute and fuzzy and whatever, though I'd never have something like a dog or cat dropping their crap all about the *Navaplastas*—that'd be like shittin' on your baby . . . but that don't mean that you should go about spending half your life tryin' to catch a glimpse of them through your binoculars when you could be doin' other things . . . like drinkin'.

But, then again, who am I to tell people how to live their lives? I'm a great big tub of guts with a big, yapping mouth and a heart of gold . . . well, those first two, not so sure about the heart of gold, between you and me.

Anyway, I picked up these three guys from a terminal out on Rudbux-3. I'd been doin' some forgettable job or other when I caught sight of them in the Interstellar Hires bay of the terminal.

Not quite sure what I expected, because they were all standin' about there, wearing safari gear, with the beige, and the hats, and, of course, the binoculars hangin' down round their necks. Two of them were tall, well, taller than me, and the other one was just a mite smaller.

I got that tingle in my large gut, the one that just about almost always steers me just fine, when I pay attention to it. Keeps me out of trouble.

I didn't pay attention to it.

"Oh, pilot? Pilot?" the tallest one called out to me.

I crammed my flabby lips together and paced over to them.

"Captain," I said, and then leaned my elbow down on a brass railing and sniffed at them.

You can tell an awful lot about a person just from sniffin'. You can get whenabouts they last had a shower—and if you're tryin' this trick, goin' about sniffin' me, then good luck—how much money they've got, and, if you're a particularly seasoned space traveller . . . or a space smuggler, like me . . . then you might even be able to work out just what planet they're from.

Don't go tellin' me that the garden-variety person can't sniff out a person from Genhawort-16. There's stories that even the dark matter gives that planet the old brushoff.

Now these guys, how I could tell they had money, was from the way they were all sweating, all over the place really, and yet they smelled totally clean. That there was *clean* sweat. And, to top that off, they also had on fresh cologne that smelled a little like honey.

Yup, I got it all decided, pretty much right there, this was a job that I might just be interested in.

Just to be sure, I looked over those features of theirs, took in those high cheekbones and those pale-blues eyes. Their complexions were pretty fair, and when I caught sight of their hands, I might've mistaken them for a little girl's, if I hadn't seen their faces too.

But I *had* seen their faces.

"Where ya goin' and how much ya payin'?" I said, keen to cut through the crap just as soon as possible.

The tallest one, who I guessed turned out to be some sort of *de facto* leaders among these guys, well he spoke first. "Captain, please allow me to introduce myself, Arghtwode"—when he said his own name he made a claw of his hand and held it at his chest —"and my two brothers: Gabriel, and Darner—Darner's the ickle one."

Now, if there's one thing that I've not heard in a long time of galaxy-running, it's the word 'ickle,' and maybe that should've been what set off my alarms even more. But—what can I say?—I'm a space smuggler and I love my credits. And I could just tell that these three 'brothers,' apparently, were just stuffed full of it.

And if I played my cards right then I could relieve them of a good portion of those credits.

I was a professional smuggler after all.

I kept my gaze all steely and fixed on the tallest one, on 'Arghtwode' as he'd introduced himself. When it comes to money, it pays to get it all sorted out right from the start . . .

Arghtwode seemed to catch my drift, or at least he'd spent just enough time with salt-of-the-earth plebs like me to have some sort of idea how to handle us, to figure out just what it was that we wanted.

Though I don't think I caught the destination all that well right then, the number of credits he spoke was good enough for me, and so I welcomed them on board the *Nava*, just as long as they didn't go touchin' anything I didn't want them to touch, of course.

. . . But when could rich people *ever* keep their hands to themselves?

2

A S I SAT at the controls of the *Nava* blasting us through space, feelin' those familiar judders of the blasters passing right through my captain's chair and breathing in all that nice, old familiar grimy greasy smell, I just propped myself up and listened to those brothers talkin' between themselves.

The tall one, Arghtwode, he was obviously the talkative one, which was to say that he was jabberin' about then, goin' on about some technical thing that I just had no patience for. Though, from what I gathered listening around the conversation, they'd all managed to cut free from their wives for the weekend and had decided to take this trip out.

They mentioned stuff about campin', and I guessed that was a good way to see animals, or whatever, though it'd never appeal to me, and I overheard them doin' some speakin' about wanting to stay there a few days.

Again, just fine by me, considering that I'd still be gettin' paid, just as a drone-controlled taxi on any planet in the Fritten System goes on chargin' while it's waitin', I'd do the same.

I'd got it pretty figured that this was gonna be one lucrative job.

Maybe I could finally upgrade the tongue scanner on the *Nava's* security systems once I got through with this job. That'd be the icing on the cake for sure.

All things considered, I was pretty glad that Arghtwode only saw his way to speaking to me whenever he had to give some directions, or to give me some info on our destination. The way I figured it, we were headed for one of those uninhabited planets just outside the rim of the Fritten System, and that was why he'd needed a smuggler. Why the brothers hadn't been able to charter some more official-sounding tour.

Though, at the time, just *why* they wanted to go to this particular planet seemed strange to me. I mean, there's a ton of planets with animals and shit all sprayed about Fritten, why didn't they just go there rather than paying someone a premium to ship them out to this particular place?

Well, as long as I was the person gettin' my fudgy meat hooks on that premium, I couldn't give less of a good Goddamn.

We drew close to the planet, to Nepheron-6, as it showed up on my navigational screen, though those brothers, or at least Arght-wode, had some technical-sounding name for it.

What did I care?

I puttered the *Nava* in through the atmosphere and brought her down *real* slow onto what, my systems assured me, was a nice bit of good solid rock.

And it was.

For once.

You have no idea how many times, for the will of a good few thousand credits, I've managed to set the *Nava* down in some sort of a shit swamp or other. And those times I'd often spend a good chunk of whatever my original fee was just to get the *Nava* approximating some kind of clean again.

And if there's one thing that I hate more than anything in this good world, it's dunking the *Nava* into some shit swamp or other . . . she deserves so much more than that.

I waited a good long time after I'd set down the landing struts, just as I'd learned all those years ago, back when I'd been a cadet in the Fritten System Authorities, checkin' to see that we *were* on some nice solid rock, and not something that was on the brink of either transformin' into a shit swamp, or wasn't about to sink into a shit swamp, or whatever.

It seemed just fine, though, since I wasn't gonna leave the ship while these brothers all trucked out to do whatever it was they were gonna do, I could quite easily lift the *Nava* up if I felt the planet givin' way or whatever.

I'd just kicked my boots back and got to restin' them on the board of controls, felt the springs all slinkin' back in my chair, and got that nice doughy, soft patch of my captain's chair all lined up with my heftier bumcheek when I noticed Arghtwode standin' at my elbow, lookin' kind of impatient.

"Captain?" he said. "We're ready when you are."

"Watcha sayin'?"

"Whenever you're ready."

"Ready for what?"

Arghtwode chuckled as if there'd been some sort of a misunderstanding, and I guess there had been, somewhere along the line. "To come out with us, along the plains. To do the *heavy* lifting."

Now, I ain't no workshy moron, nope, nothin' like that, but I sure as hell ain't no one's donkey—not for any price, though in this case, the money that was bein' paid, was most likely the only reason I didn't toss all three of those brothers right out on their ears, into that radioactive pink dust, or whatever it was, out there.

At that time I'd already got myself half asleep and dreamin' about a roast shank of somethin' or other—somethin' tasty, in any case—and only then did I notice that a strand of dribble had just gone and rolled down my chin.

I wiped it off, did my little *donkey* snort, and then eyed this Arghtwode guy nice and close. "Listen here, buddy. What we agreed, what I signed up for, was so that I'd bring you guys out here, run the risks of passin' over the limit of Fritten"—though, as I thought to myself then, the risks of breakin' the limit of Fritten was way less than they'd been all shaked up to be, though most Fritten citizens preferred to believe in the lies told them in all the media, and I'm not ashamed to say that I just played up to them . . . made some good money off them, in fact—"so just what is it that you've gotta say?"

Arghtwode's mouth curled just a little at the corners as he caught me in that glare of his. "You'd best come with us, Captain. We're prepared to pay a fair price, but you've got to remember that you're not the only one that's aware you're operating outside the zone of control of Fritten."

And just then I thought to glance up, to see the two brothers—whatever the hell their names were—holding a pair of blaster rifles, both of them pointed right at me.

Now, I'd like to say that that was the first . . . or *last* . . . time something like that happened to me. But that'd be a lie, and me ma, well, she always did her best to teach me that lyin' was the worst.

So, I let loose a long sigh, swung myself up onto my feet, and wondered at just what sort of mess I'd got into this time, and wondered just how I might be able to get myself out of it.

3

BEFORE we got ourselves off the bridge, one of Arghtwode's brothers—the 'ickle' one, if memory serves—he just did some sort of fancy thing with one of the power controls to the thrusters of the *Nava*, the ones that got us up out of the atmosphere.

That's probably one thing you should also know about space smugglers. Though we're expert at gettin' stuff— and in this case *people*—all smuggled through somewhere just fine, we're not all that greatly acquainted with the intricacies of our ships.

At least, I don't think the majority—and that includes me—would be able to pass any sort of exam on the technicalities of flyin', or nothin'. Because, and I've found this too, we seem to do way better with a blaster in our hands and not an awful lot of talkin'.

That's the smugglers' university.

And so, we all got ourselves suited up, me in the rag-tag suit I've had for a good, solid age, and which I'm not all that confident in the shielding of . . . which is to say that if that *were* radioactive dust sprinkled all over the place, most likely I was gonna be something like a nuclear reactor when we got done.

Maybe I should've spent more money on gettin' a new suit, rather than upgrading the security systems on the *Nava* for the nth time. But, as any self-respectin' space smuggler knows, you gotta make it your life's work not to set foot off your ship at any time . . . because, chances are, most likely if you're parked up in some public terminal on some shitstain of a planet—you know, just like normal?—then you can bet your last credit that some low-life smuggler's gonna steal the thing from right under your nose.

Well, out there, on Nepheron, I guessed that wasn't gonna be so much of an issue, given that it was uninhabited and all. Though that didn't mean that I didn't calibrate all the security systems like normal. Couldn't discount some smuggler runnin' on by the planet and spottin' the *Nava* all parked up there, nice and unguarded.

Bastards, smugglers, every last one of us.

Arghtwode at least decided that I wasn't all that much trouble, and those blaster rifles got slung over shoulders as we marched our way—and I *do* mean marched, because you can always tell a week-ender from the way he walks, the way he *has* to make every moment of his freedom count, before he goes back to work Monday.

Weren't much really out there on Nepheron, truth be told. A load of that pink dust all flurryin' about in a light breeze, and whatever, rattlin' up against the visor of my spacesuit. I just concentrated on the breathin' part, breathin' in that stale, iron-tasting air, and doin' my best not to breathe in too deep, knowin' that I didn't want to find myself out here askin' any one of these guys for a scrap of air.

Didn't wanna find myself askin' mercy from them in any way.

It got hot in that suit, too, from all the walkin'. And since I hadn't done all that much maintenance with the ventilator unit, my visor got foggy real quick. Moisture stuck to my face and ran down my cheeks just as bad as if I'd been cryin'. But I just kept my eyes all focussed on the heels of the brother in front, and told myself that, soon, they'd let us have a rest or somethin'.

4

THAT REST didn't come till the sun—or whatever the hell that star shinin' on Nepheron was called—began to settin'. We'd been wading through some rocky terrain for some time, these shit-brown rocks all poking up through the pink dust, and it seemed only to be gettin' rockier up ahead. I don't like to sound melodramatic, but I was gonna say *mountainous*.

Anyway, Arghtwode led us into a little dome-shaped crevice all dug out from one of the rocks, and then he set about to pitchin' up the camp. It was one of those pretty expensive-lookin' things, the things that'd most likely cost about half what I'd pitched down into the safety systems of the *Nava*, gettin' them up to the high—*high*—standards that only I could see myself.

Soon enough, we all got ourselves camped up inside that thing, and we could take off our spacesuits—*finally*—and pitch ourselves over and have a little lie down.

And, I most likely don't need to tell you, not with these flubbery guts of mine, these mounted-up double chins, but I *was* in pretty good need of a lie down. Just some downtime to get myself sorted followin' all that marchin' we'd got done that day.

I stuck up my spacesuit on the hanger that one of the brothers had somehow sprung up out of some pole or other, and I watched the moisture drippin' down off it.

The brothers had pretty much taken to ignorin' me, well they'd gone and sat off over on the other side of the tent where they all gathered about this cookin' thing, this kinda portable oven to warm themselves—because, truth be told, the temperature in the tent was pretty chilly—and they were roastin' up ersatz pork sausages.

Those herby smells just wafted about in the air, doin' some pretty black magic things to my nostril hairs, and passin' dozens of quivers through my gut.

My mouth, too, was watering away.

I caught Arghtwode's eye, and he gave me an apologetic smile, and he stooped so as not to bang his head on the ceiling of the tent as he trudged on over to me. Then he stuck out his hand, into my chest. "No hard feelings, eh, Captain?"

I stared for a long time at his hand, not because I was thinking to shake it but because I was wondering if I could get away with gnawing it to pieces right in front of him, without one of his brother gettin' all trigger happy with one a those blaster rifles.

I guessed it was better to bide my time, because if there's one thing I've learned in my time as a space smuggler it's that whenever you're about with fellow crooks—and despite their appearances, their money, and *those* accents, they *were* crooks—they always trip themselves up somewhere along the line.

Arghtwode seemed to grasp the idea soon enough that I had no idea of accepting that handshake of his. I've made it just about my life's work not to shake one more hand than I absolutely have to.

For whatever reason, I decided that now was the best time to break my silence. "What's all this heavy liftin' you talked about back on the *Nava*?"

"The *Nava*?" Arghtwode said, reluctantly letting his hand drop down by his side, and screwing up his eyes as if he was confused.

Now, if there's one sure-fire way to thoroughly piss me off, then it's by slinging shit at my ship. Right, well, you don't even have to go so far as to sling shit, because what this guy was saying, why it was enough for me to clock him with everything I'd got.

But, over his shoulder, I could still see those brothers of his still cleanin' up their rifles real nice, and I knew doin' anything rash would be a mite dumb . . . even for my numb-knuckled smuggler's brain.

"Oh," Arghtwode said, apparently catching that rage flashin' through my eyes and, most likely, noticing that I was crunchin' my fingers up into fists, "your *ship*."

"Yeah," I said, "now stop being all cute and such and tell me just what I'm in for here, why dontcha?"

Arghtwode pressed those bloodless lips of his tight together. "I don't think you're in any position to be asking any question other than 'How high?'"

I felt my chest tightening up and my heart beatin' hard, no doubt getting itself ready for a pummelling. But there just wasn't no pummelling on the cards, not with those brothers of his skulking off in the corner of the tent, and with those blaster rifles.

"Do we understand one another?" Arghtwode said, arching an eyebrow.

"Perfect," I said.

"Perfect-*ly*, I think you mean." And then he closed one eye as if thinking me over for some measurements or other—I hoped it wasn't for a noose or nothin' like that. "Where are you from, anyway?"

I gave him a little growl at the back of my throat. "None of your business."

He shrugged then half-turned away from me, headed back

towards his brothers and their rifle cleanin'. "If you're ashamed then I apologise for asking."

I growled a little more but saw there was nothing else to do at that time. They had three rifles between them, and I had nothing but my tub of guts and my thick skull. So I did what all good smugglers do in a time when there's nothin' to be done, and I turned on my side and shifted off to sleep.

5

GETTIN' WOKE UP by someone diggin' a rifle butt into your belly ain't no fun, I can tell you that for nothing. And that was just what happened to me a few hours later on. And I rolled over and looked up above me in the faint light of the tent. The light was comin' from someone's torch or some such *camper's* innovation.

The 'ickle' one was standin' over me with a good old smirk on his face, and that same arched eyebrow his brother possessed. I guessed that evil ran in the family. Or at least it did when these three boys all got together for the weekend.

"Time to get up, Captain," the ickle one said.

I did just what he said, rubbin' my head, eyes and arse, in that order, before shuffling up to my feet. Now, thing is, whatever else us space smugglers might be: somewhat sweary, always stinkin' and usually a good way to bein' honest-ta-God sober, we generally know how to snap to it at a moment's notice.

Once the sleepin's done with that's all, we're awake, and ready to go. All the travellin'—all the *workin'*—takes its toll after a while, and since we really don't got no place to cross-reference our body clock with then it kinda makes sense.

Always has done to me, in any case.

And so, with all that rubbin' done with, I was just as alert as I would've been back in my days as an FSA cadet, all bright-eyed and bushy-tailed.

The three brothers all seemed just as up and ready to go for the morning too, a bit unfortunate seein' as I'd been planning to sock them somehow, hopin' they'd be like most rich people and not so great at mornings.

Not to say I'm a morning person, not by a long shot.

And—anyway—that's a whole other story altogether.

We packed up the tent . . . or, well, I stood back in my nicely aired-out spacesuit and watched them pack up, trying not to break anything, while the ickle one kept an eye on me, and his blaster rifle very much pointed at me.

It was round that point that I noticed that great big thing that looked like a rocket launcher, that Arghtwode was carryin'. He had it hoiked over his shoulder as we broke camp and headed further into the hills. It seemed like none of the brothers were takin' so much as a sliver of a chance with me, and they all kept their rifles firm in their paws.

I just did my best to keep up with them. Don't let anyone tell you that I don't have no admiration for the jobs donkeys do, because after that ordeal I ain't got nothin' but respect for the fellas. They do alotta hikin' and take alotta grief for not much recompense.

And at least I *was* gettin' paid . . . or that was the theory.

Arghtwode led us through more and more of those hills, and I could already taste my salty dog breath comin' back at me, rebounding off the inside of my visor. Thing that's just about always bothered me about my spacesuit is that weird, sour, piss-type odour. Maybe it is piss. I got the thing second-hand, so who knows?

Still, that wasn't doin' all that much good considerin' my empty belly and all that walkin'—wasn't makin' me feel anything special in any case. I could almost taste that bile frothin' about at the back of my throat. I just pressed on all the harder, feeling all that well-won flab of mine jigglin' itself into muscles . . . or so I imagined it . . . and the *suck* and *schwee* sound as I breathed in and out in my suit.

The terrain got yet more jagged as we hurried on our way—and I do mean *hurried*—but soon enough we reached whatever Arghtwode had in mind as our destination. At that point I'd completely given up asking questions or whatever, and was just ready to take whatever the hell these brothers wanted to give me.

Things'd got so bad at that point, at least in my fudged-up brain, that I was startin' to thinking that I just didn't care all that much about the fee any longer, and woulda just been pleased to get out of the situation, to be back on the *Nava* and floatin' away someplace.

Still, didn't seem like that was an option at the time.

Arghtwode stood in front of this dirty great big cave, and by big, I mean . . . well, a good three or four storeys high, summat like that, and it did that echoey thing that all big caves usually do, which was to say that when one of the brothers—the middle one—shouted out into it, his voice came floatin' all the way back.

The echo was so loud I could even hear it inside my goldfish bowl spacesuit helmet, and I felt that scurry of nerves and stuff all janglin' up and down my spine, like I was some kid that was ascared of the dark.

It was at that point that Arghtwode turned to me, grinnin' ear to ear—the *bastard*—and said, "Well, after *you*, Captain."

I stared into the great big blackness of that cave, and then I looked to those blaster rifles all pointed at me and I let loose a long sigh, and wondered whether bummin' about the galaxy, takin' work where I could find it, was really a smart career move after all.

Well, as I took those steps towards the mouth of the cave, I considered that since it weren't much of a career at all then there just wasn't any 'move' about it neither . . .

6

I GUESSED it weren't much my place to ask just where I was headed, and what exactly my role was in all this steppin'-into-the-cave business.

As I ventured in there, I felt that glassy echo take over the helmet of my spacesuit, you know, kinda like that sound when you go to a beach and put a shell against your ear. That was what it was like. Only I also had a pretty much never-ending darkness—or *gloom*, however you'd like it—to contend with.

I noticed that the terrain below my feet got all kinda crunchy, and didn't feel all that substantial, not at all, really. But I just went on my way, sure that those brothers, that they were all awaitin' at the mouth of the cave, and sooner I got through with this, sooner we could all forget this whole thing.

I caught yet more of that pissy smell in my mouth and nostrils —funny how that smell don't never get old, no matter how accustomed you get to it—and I did my best to keep my stomach from swirling about, to keep that bile from lickin' at my throat.

As the dark got all the more thicker and deeper, I felt like I was headed down a slope. When I glanced back over my shoulder, I saw that the mouth of the cave was only a faint glimmer of pink, and though I guessed the dust below my feet was still pink, like the dust out on the planet, I had no way of seein' it.

And it was round then when I heard a pretty thick, and pretty *angry*, roar.

7

NOW, all told, there really ain't that much that really throws my spine out of place, but gettin' roared at out from the dark, well that might very well be one of those things.

Just sayin'.

One thing that I've got a good sense of, though, in all my space smuggling, is for danger. I know just when it's time to hit the ground, when it's time to give up on whatever scrap of bravery's left inside of me, and just make like a seven-year-old girl.

And so that's what I did then, minus the girly scream . . . or at least no one could hear my girly scream comin' out from my helmet, or from that deep down in the cave.

And why did I care all that much about what those brothers thought about me anyhow?

With my helmet pressed down into that dust, I felt the vibrations throbbin' through the ground, and that distinctive poundin' sound that can only be from a monster. And, let me tell you, I've come across just enough monsters in my time to know one.

Thing is, with monsters, is you've gotta just stay as still as possible, and do your level best not to freak out. All things considered, all that had happened to me on the job so far, I think I kept things pretty much under wraps.

Kept myself from freakin' out too much.

Sure, there was one point where I was sure I might get eaten, or at least stepped on. It was just as that throbbin' reached its loudest, and that vibrating got so hard that I could feel it rockin' my brain about my skull.

Maybe I said a prayer then, maybe I didn't.

Guess that's the beauty of bein' a sole operator, sometimes. You get to be just as heroic or unheroic as you damn-well please.

And I please damn-well a hell of a lot of the time, be sure of that.

Anyway, said monster, he just kept on shippin' out of the cave, rising his great big paws—whatever they looked like—and then his steppin' got all quiet, and I knew it was safe for me to get up from where I'd thrown myself down.

For some reason, dunno why, I brushed away the dust stickin' to my spacesuit. Guess at times even a space smuggler has to draw the line somewhere on personal appearance.

Then, pretty soon after, I heard a lotta howlin' and bustin' coming from the mouth of the cave, and I guess my good friend Mister Monster had just met those clients of mine.

I don't mind sayin' that I enjoyed a good, smug smile at that time.

Just for a few minutes or so.

8

I SNUCK my way back out of the cave, keepin' to the shadows, pretty anxious not to get myself spotted by Mister Monster if he decided to do a one-eighty and come rattlin' back through the cave all hungry and pissed right off.

When I reached the mouth of the cave there was still a great bunch of whoopin' and screechin' going on—never tell *me* that them upper-class folk know how to keep a lid on their enthusiasm —and I poked my head out to see just what they'd got themselves up to.

Mighty nice beastie, he was. About as tall as ten men, and three times as thick. Kinda looked like a dinosaur now, thinkin' about it. All scaly and such. I guessed he'd have to have some pretty mean natural armour to see off the radiation, or whatever nasty they had on this planet here.

Most notable, though, was the lack of eyes, and how Mother Nature—or whoever the hell ran things about here—had kinda compensated with those giant jaws, and those bone-crunchin' teeth.

Well, I guess the next thing that happened was my mouth latched all the way down, so much so that it probably accounts for that crackin' sound I get from my jaw when I go to bite a chunk of somethin' that most likely could do with a bit of choppin' before getting anywhere near being ready to pass my lips.

Next thing that happened was I noticed the three brothers had all netted the thing with that bazooka—or whatever it was—of Arghtwode's. And now the monster was pinned between the three of them, just roarin' and gettin' pissed off some more, and occasionally whippin' its pointy—but apparently none-too-sharp—claws at the net trappin' it where it was.

Right about then, I twigged that, apparently in the excitement of the beastie poking its head out of its cave, of comin' to join the party, the brothers had all left their rifles down in the pink dust. *Way* too far for them to snatch up all quick, and definitely not easy gettin' if they had any wish to keep that beastie pinned in that net of theirs.

I guessed they'd also banked on that beastie having chewed up a great big load of space smuggler, and thought me all taken care of.

Maybe it had the good sense to sniff me out back in the cave, and took that good old decision just to maybe skip the appetiser, that there were some pretty clean-smellin' boys right outside and waitin' for it.

Guess I got to feelin' something for that beastie or, at least, got to seein' just where it was coming from.

And so, quick as I could, before the situation all upped on changed on me, as it quite often has a habit of doin', I rushed over to the first rifle I saw—the one I guessed the 'ickle' brother had dropped—and I snatched it up and bellowed, top of my lungs, "Right you, divs, you hold it right there, why dontcha?!"

Lookin' back on it, it was pretty funny seein' all those beleaguered glances of theirs, those total looks of surprise as they got the idea that they were pinned down, that if they wanted to come after me then they'd need to let go of that well-pissed-off little—though not *so* little, thinking on it—beastie they had nice and trapped there.

I made a point of searchin' out Arghtwode and givin' him one of my nicest, sweetest smiles. One that he'd just keep nice and etched on his mind for the rest of his life.

However long that'd be.

Funnily enough, Arghtwode had enough guts about him to call out to me, from the other side of that beastie, where I could see the rope of the net already beginnin' to wane, just a little, in his grasp. "What do we do now?" he said.

"*We?*" I said. "Can't see that *we* are really gonna be doin' anythin' much. You sincerely can't see your way to thinkin' up anything that might sound good to us all?"

Then something in Arghtwode's expression seemed to snap right open, and his voice got all twitchy, all *snarly*. Surely that same voice he used with his brothers, to keep them in check, to make them know that *he* was the leader of the pack.

Guess, all things told, I was growin' a mite weary of Arghtwode by that time.

"Listen here, *you!* You better shoot this beast dead right this moment or I'll make it my life's work to track you down and have you killed."

"You really know how to romance a stranger," I said, and squeezed the grip of that blaster rifle all the tighter. "Think I know just how this is gonna play, for all us."

Arghtwode's eyes flared and his mouth became a mewling pit.

"What's gonna happen," I said, "is I'm gonna go ship outta here, and you lot can all wait round here till someone comes and rescues you. How's that sound? Guess your wifies could see their way to bailin' you out, and all."

Now, if there's one thing that the self-respecting upper-classer really hates—especially the safari kind—it's havin' to owe anything at all to a woman. You try it sometime. See if they'll let a woman cough up for dinner, or even go Dutch, never gonna happen.

Cad's a cad, you see?

And don't even start to get talkin' about havin' them put in that situation with their *wife*.

Arghtwode got a little more irritate, if that was at all humanly possible . . . and I think Arghtwode just went on to prove it was. So maybe it was a good thing that it was his ickle brother who spoke up next, and threw a tiny spanner into the works.

"What about your ship?" the ickle brother said. "I've disabled the afterburners, you won't get up into space till I sort them out."

I felt my gut tighten a bit, but that blaster rifle still felt as good as it had all along, and I pointed it at him just to make me feel a little better about the state of things. Think I saw him give a little gulp too. "Still," I said, "someone'll pass by sooner or later, and I have to say I'd feel a shot more snug up in my ship, dozin' away and knowin' you boys are still out here all tied up with this monster of yours."

That sent Ickle Brother's face all blank once again, not to say his muscles a ripplin' from holdin' onto that net holding down the beastie so tight.

Just on cue, that beastie let loose a right-old rip of a roar, and I watched them all quiverin' in their spacesuits, their attention just as fast movin' off me and goin' to the beastie.

I collected up the other two rifles and slung them over my shoulder for good measure. I have to admit that I'd developed something of a soft spot for that monster there, he'd done me no harm, and I saw these fellas doin' him some harm being not right by a long shot.

And so, with a final wave to the brothers, and especially to Arghtwode, still smouldering away there, his cheeks red as roses beneath that visor of his, I swept on out, leavin' those boys there in the lurch.

Leaving them to their weekend plans.

Just the boys, all hangin' round.

That was what they wanted, weren't it?

9

EVEN ME, with my lardy arse, and loadin' three rifles to boot, made it back to the *Nava* before the sun set that evening, which wasn't to say that I didn't have sweat crawling out of every known orifice of my body . . . not to count the ones I *don't* know about.

And, just as true to what I'd said to those three as they pinned back that beastie, I dialled up a distress call, shuffled my feet up onto my control panel, and rested my head back, ready to have a good old sleeple.

I got a reply pretty soon, all things told, a passing small freighter ship with this nervous-eyed pilot stopped by. And he had all good reason to be nervous, what with being outside of Fritten in a known pirating spot, but he stopped anyway.

I appreciated that.

He knew a lot more about my ship than I did, not unusual at all, and he fixed me up pretty good before my conscience got the better of me and I tipped him off about those three brothers all of them off with a netted beastie, and he told me he'd go off to do whatever he could.

Last thing I knew of those three was when I was blastin' my way back over the frontier, headed back into Fritten, out of madness, and back into what passes for sense in this universe, when I got the call through from the pilot of the freighter.

Said he'd picked up three mightily pissed-off guys all dressed up in safari clothes and such. And that he'd got them to let loose the beastie, and it'd shucked back off into its cave, without taking a bite out of any of them brothers.

Wasn't quite sure how to feel about that.

But I know just how to feel about the bag full of credits they left behind on the bridge of the *Nava*, way more than my fee for the job, but—what the hell—I reckoned, I'd done way more beyond the call of duty.

And, what's more, they were such lubbardly cowards.

THE DISGUISED SOUND

1

THE *FUZZ* of a glitching 'bot band is too much even for a space smuggler's ears.

How there're people who enjoy it really beats me.

I gripped on tighter to my moiser—my moisturised alcohol—as I squeezed my way through all the bundled-up bodies, leaving the on-stage 'bots to their digital psychobabble.

As I passed through, without having to look too closely, I could tell that most everyone in the club was kids. The reason I didn't have to look *too* closely was based on the fact that most of them wore those garish, light-up t-shirts which were probably only in fashion sometime around the turn of the century . . . so about the time I was an adolescent—*har, har*.

Nobody my age, or closing on my age, would have dared to wear those.

Most of them had piercings, too; something which'd drifted out of style *decades* ago, but which was apparently making a rapid comeback.

Tattoos, also, seemed to have turned into the new norm, and, for once, I was glad to have my flabby appearance, and the implied need to cover it up with my space-smuggler standard—beaten leather jacket over the top of space thermals. Not having tattoos myself, I didn't want to come across as some kind of 'square' to these kids, after all.

Once I'd got myself clear of the *fuzz* hacking through the air—though I'd yet to get it shaken completely out of my skull—I turned my attention to the job at hand . . . to the reason I'd come to this bar called the *Seven Severed Skulls* in the first place.

There was only *one* reason.

And that reason was *credits*.

A prospective client of mine had been gnawing at my ear for the longest time, wanting to meet so that we might discuss a job. To be honest, I probably would've blown them off if it hadn't been for the sweet numbers quoted.

I wonder if anyone ever wrote a book on the etiquette of turning down large sums of money . . . seems to me that there should be one.

I got through to the bar area, and found myself confronting yet more kids in those garish, glowing t-shirts. I had more beady, glaring eyes staring back at me from various animal tattoos than I would've found if I'd gone and crash landed in the fog swamps of Yunthaul-7.

All the tables were taken, of course; this being a Friday night, and getting on for tenth hour.

I did a quick scan of the room, trying to work out if there was anybody looking suspicious enough to be a prospective client of mine.

Finally I found him.

Or, as I probably should've said, I found *her*.

As I approached, I couldn't help feeling just the slightest bit flabbergasted at the way in which *she* looked suspicious here. It wasn't in the normal manner, which would be to say, the way that I appeared here; looking several decades too old to be safely allowed in through the doors of *Seven Severed Skulls*. No, this woman, if she'd wanted to, despite being perhaps five or ten years over the unspoken age limit, could easily have fit in. But, first of all, she was sat at the fringes; making a point of not engaging with anybody. And then there was the fact that she was dressed differently:

No glowing t-shirt.

No tats on show.

She wore a pair of overalls which made it look like she'd just got off her shift.

And her hair was cropped into a sensible cut, hanging down just beneath the earlobes.

In short, she *stuck out* just as much as I did.

Our eyes met as I was about half a dozen paces away, and I gave her a polite nod.

She nodded back and then glanced about swiftly in that way which never fails to unsettle me . . . to make me feel that there might be somebody watching our meeting from the wings. Sure enough, when I followed her gaze, I saw this guy in a leather trench coat, collar turned up to hide his neck, and a baseball cap pulled *way* down to cover his forehead, eyes and nose.

Bad News.

That was what this situation said to me.

But—*hell*—it wasn't like I was going to turn down good pay.

Not when I'd nearly deafened myself as part of the deal of meeting with my prospective client here.

I got right to it when I slipped on down into her booth, slumping my body onto the cushion beside her. "Who's that by the door?"

She flinched, glanced over to the door, then looked back at me. "Uh, no one."

I rolled my eyes, then looked over to the guy in the trench coat. "You sure it's 'no one'?"

"Um-hmm," she replied, and then reached for her drink, sitting on the table.

She took a long swig, and I saw that she was trembling as she did so.

When she finally replaced the drink—this thick, bluish-looking concoction—she looked me right in the eyes and tried out that shy smile of hers once again.

"Captain Wright," she said. "It's a pleasure to meet you."

She held out her hand to me.

I took it from her.

Her skin was soft, and *fleshy* . . . the type which has had near enough every cream and powder bestowed upon it. Skin like that doesn't come without a hefty price in terms of credits, effort and time.

"Wish I could say the same," I replied, "but you haven't told me what you're called."

"Oh, right," she said, again flashing that nervous smile. "Ellery," she said, her eyes once more drifting to that trench-coated figure at the door, then back to me. "Ellery Templeton."

"Well, Miss Templeton—"

"Ellery—*Ellie*."

"Fine, *Ellie*; what's this job you want me to do?"

Again, though, 'Ellie' was off staring to the door of the place, looking at that trench-coated wonder once more.

"Look, here," I said, straightening up in my seat, squeezing in my gut just as far as it would go. "If you're gonna play games here, then there's stuff I gotta . . ."

She reached out and took hold of my forearm with some quite sharp fingernails.

It made me tingle . . . just a little.

"Wait, Captain!" she said, her voice a stifled whisper in my ear.

I met her eyes.

The colour of dusty rubies.

"He's gone," she said.

I looked to the door.

Saw that she was telling the truth.

"Now," she said, her voice still low, and the damp warmth of her breath up against my earlobe. "Now we can talk about the job."

2

"CAPTAIN. Would you like another drink?"

"Uh, sure," I replied.

I watched on as my client—*Ellie*—refilled my moiser; almost to the rim.

She gave me a pleasant, stranger's smile and then wandered off.

I have to admit that, in all my years of space smuggling, that's one of those trigger phrases. The kind that gets my muscles tightening up, and my stomach a touch queasy.

From personal experience, the clients who wind up using space smugglers tend to act as stingy as possible. Oh, it doesn't matter if they're the richest man, woman or kid in the universe; it's just this sort of mental block where they equate handing over a fat wad of credits to a smuggler as being some kind of damning reflection on themselves. And the same goes for offering a smuggler complimentary drinks. *Anything* complimentary, for that matter.

I peered down into the refilled glass before me, and then out through the porthole of my client's spaceship cruiser to the blackness blasting on by.

I thought about how Ellie had gone and changed beyond recognition when that trench-coated fellow had skedaddled. Then again, as it turned out, that trench-coated fellow *was* the entire job. As Ellie had explained to me, the guy in the trench coat was an alien.

Or, to tell the truth, I'd intuited that from around the edges.

She'd fed me some crap about him being 'special' or 'immaterial' . . . it all boiled down to the very same thing, even when it wasn't said aloud.

Now, despite the fact that aliens exist in this—*extremely sizeable*—universe, and, perhaps, for many a universe alongside; below, above, and beyond, they tend to steer as clear as they possibly can from humans. They have their own dimensions; their own interpretations of space and time.

Good on them, is all I have to say about aliens.

If I'd have had the good fortune to be born into some other race then I'd have kept my nose clean—humankind speaking—just as well as I possibly could. My mission, if I chose to accept it, was to drag this old alien to some kind of a portal for him to use to get back . . . or to *go* . . . just wherever the hell it was that he was going.

I'm not one of those gossipy smugglers; I'm more the kind that's glad to take the money and run—to leave the asking of questions and the gazing of navels till I'm sat in the pub with the cash in my pocket.

I stretched my legs out, feeling a hundred and one things go *pop* and *crack* as I did so. For another time, perhaps with the fresh buzz of a new glass of moiser in my hand, I took in the large quarters surrounding me. 'Large' was, most likely, an understatement.

The truth of the thing was that the area was large enough to stash the entirety of my own spaceship: the *Navaplastas*. Aside from the *Nava* parked up across from us, there wasn't an awful lot. I could easily imagine that, in this ship's heyday, this area could quite easily have been used for the higher-paying travellers; the whole place furnished as any kind of paradise that might be wished for. It seemed a little sad to me that a cruiser like this one had obviously fallen upon such hard times. These ships used to be the very picture of elegance all throughout the universe, and, well, to see it now being used for such *illicit* purposes did tug a mite at the heartstrings.

I had toyed with the notion of going off and sitting in the captain's seat of the *Nava* while this cruiser blasted us along, but had had the notion struck down by Ellie because she wanted me to be 'ready'. She wanted me to have my space blaster to hand, ready to fight back if we found ourselves getting into any sort of trouble . . . although she had claimed that she was most worried about space pirates, I could tell—from her tone of voice, the way that she held her shoulders rigid—that it was something else entirely.

For one, if she really *was* afraid of space pirates then she would've had me in the *Nava* right from the off—most likely flying alongside the cruiser. That way I would've been ready, at a snap of the fingers, to take up against any prospective pirates. To get after them with the *Nava's* laser cannons.

For two, if space pirates had been the real issue, and my role was in protecting the cruiser from them, then Ellie would never have been dosing me up with the quantity of moiser that she was.

Now, I grant that there're some things which just aren't received wisdom outside of smuggler circles, but I'd always imagined that 'shooting while sober' had always been somewhere near the top of the common-sense list. Then again, if there's one thing I've learned in all my years of trawling from system to system, from galaxy to galaxy, it's that humans can recreate *Stupid* in all of a hundred thousand million different ways.

No, I got it clear into my head that there was definitely something up.

And, likely as not, I was going to get to the bottom of it.

Because it would make all the difference about whether or not I went paid at the end of the job.

Right as I was sipping at the rim of my moiser, and thinking about breaking this bout of inaction, before Fate did me the favour; I felt a harsh throbbing sensation pass all the way through the cruiser. In my mind, I planned the route of the impact, and the resulting shock, and saw it travelling all the way along the prow.

I don't quite know which came first, if I made up my mind to leave my comfortable seat—and moiser—behind, or if the impact made the decision for me.

In the end, though, I found myself staggering from side to side, attempting to find my balance, as I headed for the doorway out into the corridor.

3

I WAS SURPRISED to find the bridge entirely empty. The half dozen or so seats all arranged about the view screen, looking out onto our pathway into the stars, vacated.

As I trudged my way past a few of the screens, I saw that they were all operating on automatic input. I realised then that this cruiser had been retrofitted with some central navigation CPU or other so there'd be no need for a physical crew.

Funny to think how things have changed over the years.

Sometimes I wonder if our ancestors anticipated—like, *truly* anticipated—the extent of computer involvement in the everyday running of our lives.

As I was taking in the navigational screen, another of the vibrations passed up through the ship.

Just in time, I reached out and grabbed hold of the back of the chair in front of me, sinking my fingers into its plush, leathery surface.

From the feel of the impact, I imagined us entering some kind of an atmosphere, but I couldn't see any sign of a nearby planet on the navigational screen . . . of course, that was by no means fool proof considering our cargo. We might have passed through some wormhole, or some such, which'd sent us onto an entirely different plane.

The thing with aliens is that they're unpredictable.

And, living the life of a space smuggler, unpredictable can get you killed.

Or, worse, it can lose you money . . .

As the juddering continued, I eased my way across the length of the bridge and then over to a wall screen which showed off a readout of the souls currently aboard the cruiser.

I read off the names. There was only one: 'Ellery Templeton'.

It was then that I saw she was making her way along the corridor. Approaching the bridge.

I found myself reaching for my thigh holster, slipping my blaster free and setting it to charge.

From experience, I knew that people could get somewhat riled when a ship comes in for a spot of turbulence.

However, when Ellie did pass in through the doorway, I saw that her expression was calm.

She seemed almost *devoid* of emotion, in fact, as she said, "Follow me, please, Captain."

And, with a final glance back over my shoulder, to the eerily empty bridge of the cruiser, I did as she asked.

... She *was* the one paying after all ...

4

ELLIE LED ME up to the seventh deck of the cruiser.

As we walked, I noted that there seemed to be no kind of internal transportation system. I supposed it was down to the decrepit condition of the cruiser; that it hadn't had much love over the past decade or so. All the same, I felt myself begin to sweat buckets, and was constantly wiping my brow with the sleeve of my leather jacket. Finally, Ellie brought us out to an observation deck on the stern of the ship. All that I could see beyond was a whole bunch of space.

Nothing but stars.

I turned to her, and then realised that the trench-coated figure was standing in the doorway to the corridor behind us. I had to admit that I didn't much enjoy his habit of sneaking up, or away, whenever the feeling caught him.

"I was worried you'd gone," Ellie said. "When I couldn't find you with your ship."

I furrowed my brow. "Gone *where?*"

I thought about adding the qualifier that I wasn't likely to go *anywhere* without the *Nava* . . . what did she expect me to do, hitch a ride out on one of the evacuation capsules?

Not likely.

For a start, I've never been one for making do with dried-up rations, which is all that's stowed away on those evacuation capsules. And the less said about the bathroom situation, the better . . .

Don't let anyone tell you that space smugglers are *unclean* individuals.

Ellie gripped the brass railing which stood before the observation deck screen, and she stared out into the emptiness of space. "I thought you might have given up—that you might've grown bored."

"Yeah," I replied, "or maybe you got me drunk enough that I started to have second thoughts." I jerked my thumb over my shoulder. "What's *company* here doing?"

" 'Company' ?" Ellie said, in a whimsical voice, which, quite frankly, concerned me. "Oh"—she glanced off to the trench-coated guy, and then looked back to me—"yes, I think now should be the time."

"The time for what?"

But Ellie let go of the brass railing and strode her way across the deck, towards the doorway.

"The time for *what*?" I repeated.

But she simply slipped on out, past the trench-coated figure.

Now, if that moiser had begun to get the better of me—*it hadn't*—then I might've done something rash at that moment in time. Perhaps I would've recognised the fact that I was very much trapped where I stood, and thought quick about moving off the spot—about blazing on past that trench-coat guy . . . in other words, getting myself as far away from this stern observation deck, and the trench-coat guy, as was humanly possible.

But since I was thinking as straight as it gets, I stood my ground.

Waited.

I stared at the shadow nestled within the upturned collar of the leather trench coat, attempting to divine some sort of shape or recognisable feature.

But I saw nothing.

Once Ellie's footsteps had completely faded down the corridor, I couldn't help but start getting a touch antsy. "So," I said, "what's this about then, pal?"

No response from the trench-coat guy.

Quelle surprise.

I wondered if he was even looking at me—if the *alien* was even taking any sort of notice of me. For all I knew, his mind was off on some planet a billion light-years away. No doubt whipping through something infinitely more compelling than yours truly.

On a whim, I reached down and rested my palm on the grip of my laser blaster.

It wouldn't hurt to be ready.

To *just* be ready.

No reaction from Mr Trench Coat.

My trigger finger started to get itchy.

I tried not to think about it.

And failed.

Maybe ten minutes went by with the two of us locked in . . . well, whatever you might've called *that* standoff . . . and then I took a noble step forward.

Then another.

A shred of confidence tickled me.

Perhaps this would go just fine.

Maybe this alien would see reason.

That he wouldn't kill me, for whatever reason he had to, no doubt, kill me.

When I'd got within about half a dozen paces of Mr Trench Coat, I halted, held out my hand, and then said, "Howdy, pleased to meet you. Arkle Wright, Captain of the *Navaplastas*, you got it down in the basement."

I even threw in a wry—*I thought*—friendly smirk for good measure.

No dice.

Nothing.

Maybe another minute passed when I decided to whip my hand back, and to replace it where it had been on the grip of my blaster. "Well," I said, "guess you've got a different way of doing things wherever it is you're from . . ."

I trailed off, hoping the alien would fill in the gap with his place of origin.

But, nope.

With a sigh, I glanced about the deck.

If this alien did plan on killing me, and I was fairly certain he did, then he was certainly making something of a meal of it; making me sweat out every one of my last moments.

In the end, it was really out of a whim that I reached for the leather of the trench coat, for one of the buttons which did it up. When my fingertips touched on the polished-up plastic, I felt a pang of childish danger pass through me. That feeling of a ripple passing over the surface of the skin. My natural urge was to whip my hand back immediately. But I forced myself to keep touching.

The alien didn't seem to care either way.

He didn't *say* anything, at least.

Working carefully, I gently eased the button out from its hole.

The trench coat opened a hair.

And, for a single, blink-and-you'd-miss-it moment, I stared into an infinite, inky blackness.

It was all over in a second because an inexplicable—and *unbearable*—sound fizzed through the air of the observation deck.

Sending me to my knees.

5

TO TRY and describe that sound would be something like idiocy.

It was kind of like a combination of all the human screams, all the scrapings of paintwork, all the nasal, uncontrollable *whines* of failing engines that could possibly be mustered into a single sound.

To put it another way, it was the very worst sound I'd ever heard.

For the longest time, down there on my knees, hands covering my ears, I thought the sound would physically *rip* me apart. But I —*somehow*—remained stitched together.

The only reason I didn't remain there, down on my knees, for the best part of the rest of eternity, was because my kneecaps themselves began to ache horribly . . . you don't want to know just how many times a smuggler is forced into wearing out his knees; whether it's to fix a leaky faucet, or because somebody's poking a blaster at your temple.

As I gently leaned back, onto my sizeable buttocks, keeping my hands still pressed over my ears, I looked to the trench coat, and saw that the place I'd unbuttoned remained as it had been. There was still no sign of a person within . . . *an alien* . . . although that was really the last thing on my mind at that particular moment in time.

What was on my mind was wanting—*very much*—to shut that noise off.

And for good.

Hoping that I'd got over the worst of the ruckus, I continued to hold my hands over my ears and trudged on up to Mr Trench Coat. When I realised what I would have to do next, a tremor ran down my spine. But I primed myself. There was no other way about it. I needed to use at least one hand to replace the button in its hole.

Working steadily, pressing my tongue hard against the back of my teeth, I removed one hand from my ear and reached out to replace the button.

The noise was excruciating . . . like *impossible* to stand.

But I resisted.

By the time I had got the button back into place, and the noise had stopped, I could taste blood in my mouth from where I'd bitten into my tongue, doing my best to stand the racket.

A sudden, severe ringing occupied the entirety of my skull, seeming to send my brain slopping back and forth in the confined space.

I stared into the darkness, between the upturned collar of the trench coat, and I wondered, very clearly to myself, *Just what the hell have we got here?*

6

AS THINGS TURNED OUT, I didn't have all that much time to put my imagination to work because Ellie returned along the corridor.

I turned a, less-friendly, smirk in her direction when she walked on in. "That the old routine, huh?" I said. "You know, you could easily go scaring a guy to death with those sorts of tactics."

Either interpreting my smirk as a *genuine* smile, or else glad that she'd got what she'd wanted—that her plan had nicely geared into place—she grinned back at me. "It's the only way to show you what it's really like . . . what we're dealing with here."

"And just what *are* we dealing with here?" I said, hearing as if a thousand out-of-tune bells were all being struck in my headspace . . . all at the same time.

Ellie's grin faded a touch, and then it became an almost outright look of disappointment, the corners of her mouth turning down. "Captain, I thought that it would be plain to see."

"Yeah?" I replied. "Well, I'm not really the *plain* kind . . . I need shit spelled out for me—A-B-C style, you know? In case you were wondering, there's not all that many entry requirements to become a smuggler."

"This, Captain, is one of the many wonders of our universe."

"*Our* universe?"

She nodded. "Yes, Captain, it's the personification, the *animation*, of a pure sound."

I eyed Mr Trench Coat. "Not much of a sound, if you ask me."

She simply fed me a weak smile which told me, in no uncertain terms, to shut the hell up. "I brought you out here so that I might show you. It would have been too dangerous to release the sound somewhere more populous. It could easily interfere with the communications."

"No shit, Sherlock—then why'd you think that my *ears* were fair game?"

" 'Fair game' ?" she replied, head cocked to one side, as if idioms weren't her thing . . . for all *I* knew they weren't. She went on. "I acquired this ship, this out-of-service cruiser, about a year ago now. I was planning on starting up a catering business, you know, for weddings, Christenings, that sort of thing."

I pondered on this for a moment, knowing well about those cruisers—or 'buffets in the sky', as I thought of them to myself—and how they trucked all over the universe, delivering here or there, bringing, no doubt, a certain kind of delight to a certain kind of people. Like a lot of things in this world, me and these 'buffets in the sky' had never really had much reason to cross paths.

Until now, apparently.

I turned my attention back to Mr Trench Coat. "I don't see how that explains this *sound*."

"When I acquired the cruiser, I had a group of maintenance men look it over. I even personally inspected the craft. But it's impossible to catch absolutely everything, and so, I suppose that the sound was on board when I *bought* the ship."

"Yeah, or maybe one of those maintenance men wanted to play a practical joke."

Although I have had my personal run-ins with maintenance men—ones who I always go to great lengths to have *carefully* vetted before allowing them aboard the *Nava*—I couldn't quite get my head around them pulling a practical joke as elaborate as this one clearly was.

Unless it was a case of them having found something weird and—apparently—unfathomable, and deciding to set it free on some unsuspecting customer.

Looking at Ellie, at her spindly, almost emaciated frame; her tiny height; and her girlish blond hair dangling down about the sides of her head; it wasn't difficult to see her as a victim. Then again, I knew, more often than not, the ones who seem most likely to be victims often have the fiercest of bites . . . out of necessity they have to *protect* themselves somehow. Hiding under a table usually isn't an option . . . something I should know, being the prime coward in the universe . . .

Ellie looked to Mr Trench Coat, and then back at me. "I can't shake it. It's no use. Wherever I go, whenever I attempt to escape, it's always there . . . *following* me."

Even for me, someone who you wouldn't be remiss to call 'seedy', I could appreciate the creepiness of that statement; and the obvious complications which it brought about. I decided it was my turn to attempt a contribution to the conversation—I *was* on the clock, after all.

"Have you tried shooting it?"

Ellie's eyes widened. Either in surprise or in revelation. Before I could decide which, I whipped my blaster free of its holster, then fired off an even handful of shots at Mr Trench Coat.

All I got for my trouble was the stink of burning leather, a few melting, smoking holes in the jacket, and some scattered, piercingly acute sounds ripping through the air.

I dropped my blaster, heard it *clatter* at my feet, and brought my hands back up to their familiar position—covering my ears. I stood there, like some kind of a maniac, for several minutes. When I looked to Ellie, I saw that she was doing the same thing. I wondered how we were going to shut it off. Ellie, though, it seemed, already had the answer.

She shifted back out into the corridor, returning a minute or so later with a whole roll of—what looked, to me like—linoleum tiling . . . the stuff that most people use to cover up their kitchen floors . . . and which some of the more *Dandy* of smugglers use in their ships.

Soon enough, Ellie had Mr Trench Coat all wrapped up.

When I tested bringing my palms away from my ears, I realised that the sound had been severely dampened. I turned to Ellie, said, "Worth a go, I suppose."

"Yes," Ellie said, placing the roll of linoleum to one side.

The two of us continued to stare at Mr Trench Coat for a long while, the sound which'd been emitted following my blaster shots now nothing but a faint echo; almost imperceptible.

And certainly not—*now*—doing any harm.

I looked to Ellie again, sure that I'd found the answer. "How about blasting it out into space?"

Ellie shook her head. "No, I've tried that a few times; all that happens is that it's gone for, perhaps, a few hours, a *day* at the most, and then it returns . . . to *watch* me."

I puzzled this out, thinking of all the ways animate beings have been 'dealt with' throughout the ages of human civilisation. And I came up blank.

It seemed as if there was nothing to be done for Mr Trench Coat.

I slipped Ellie a sidelong glance. "Listen, I appreciate the work, and all, but I can't help wondering just why you thought that I'd be any help at all in terms of getting shot of this thing?"

Ellie remained silent.

Her expression stone-faced.

And it was then I noted the strange lightness at my thigh.

Where my blaster was . . . I reached for it; felt nothing . . . where my blaster *had been* holstered.

It was then that I saw Ellie holding my own blaster at my chest.

A certain *fire* in her eyes.

"I thought this would be worth a go," she said. "I haven't tried *this* before."

"Now," I said, managing to raise a nervous smile from somewhere, "what's all this *about*? I mean, you think it'll start following *me*? What about if you shoot me dead, huh? What'll happen then?"

Ellie shrugged. "I'll find another smuggler with more greed than brain; run through this little routine again until I can realise it to my satisfaction."

That seemed to be the last card I had to play, so there was nothing much remaining for me except to gulp, and watch Ellie slinking from the observation deck, along the corridor, and—apparently—off the ship.

I looked to Mr Trench Coat, and, perhaps, he looked back at me.

7

I WONDERED if Ellie thought she'd snatch the *Nava*, go blasting out into space . . . it would certainly be preferable to floating through space in an evacuation capsule waiting for some Good Samaritan to pick her up. Even despite the situation, despite the fact that I was stuck up on the observation deck with Mr Trench Coat, and that I might find myself with a companion for life, I smirked at the thought that Ellie would so much as manage to get *one* of the *Nava's* doors open.

To do so, she'd have to go through a whole cascade of security measures.

And, even if she got lucky, she'd trip up eventually.

Even though I was fairly confident about the *Nava's* security, I kept an eye on the observation screen, worried that my worst fears might be realised; and that I'd see Ellie shooting off into space in the cockpit of the *Nava*. There can't be anything more dispiriting for a smuggler than to see his own ship for the last time, and even less to see that it's being flown by someone else.

Better to go down in flames than to have *that* . . .

It was then that the solution struck me.

I moved quickly, away from Mr Trench Coat.

I felt a tingle pass over the surface of my skin to *feel* that he might be watching me.

Once out in the corridor of the cruiser, I made my way off toward the bridge.

I got there in maybe ten minutes.

At the bridge, I stood over the controls, considering my next move.

It was then that I caught sight of the navigational display.

I screwed up my eyes, made out the dot moving away—*quite quickly*—from the cruiser.

Without needing to look twice, I could tell it was the *Nava*.

My heart throbbed in my throat. I felt a shaking take over my entire body.

But I held myself still.

Made myself think clearly.

Here I was, with my *own* ship.

A cruiser, no less.

I'd had a go steering one of these a long while ago, and it hadn't gone all that badly . . . not out in space, anyway. The issues had come when I'd brought us down into atmosphere—but everybody's got their beginner's story . . .

It was easier than I imagined to disengage the CPU which was controlling the cruiser, and I set the navigational systems to tail the *Nava*. I knew that this cruiser would have enough punch in it to stay close. I suppose one advantage the usurped captain has that he knows *all about* his own ship; just about the most thoroughly explored subject in his mind. Even as I thought it, it made my heart swell into a knot, but if there's one area where the *Nava* falls down it's in her manoeuvrability. She ain't one of those drop-into-atmosphere ships. She needs the slow-and-easy treatment.

Already, eyeing the navigational screen, I could tell that Ellie was putting in some effort to get the engines sizzling . . . no doubt hoping to make some serious distance before my dumb smuggler's brain put together the vaguest notion of a plan.

She obviously hadn't thought that I'd break free of my inner-caveman so quick.

That's me all over.

Full of surprises.

I allowed myself a slight smirk as I saw the cruiser gaining on the *Nava*—just sheer, brute-force strength tugging us on its coat tails. I turned to take in the rest of the bridge.

I don't know particularly what I was expecting—perhaps a high-five from one of the non-existent members of the crew for my heroics of chasing down the *Nava*?—but when I looked, I saw that Mr Trench Coat was standing in the doorway.

Watching me.

I felt a chill enter my bloodstream.

But I put it out of my mind.

And turned all my attention to chasing down Ellie.

To chasing down my own ship.

8

I T TOOK the best part of a day to fully rein in the *Nava*, and, when I finally did, I really couldn't think what to do next. I suppose I was hoping something would strike me. But all I could think about was the laser cannons this cruiser was packing, and that, if I chose to go that route, I would be shooting down my very own ship. Not to mention sending Mr Trench Coat on my trail for the rest of my days. No, what I needed was something more ingenious.

Something which Ellie wouldn't see coming.

As I spun on through another series of navigational screens, it came to me.

I worked quickly, turning side-on to squeeze past Mr Trench Coat.

I jogged down the corridor—that's right, *jogged*—until I reached the escape capsules.

When I glanced back, I saw, as I'd planned, that Mr Trench Coat had followed.

I jabbed the controls for the escape capsules, calibrating a pair of them.

One for me.

One for Mr Trench Coat.

That done, I turned my attention to Mr Trench Coat.

Not knowing what to do, I gestured to the opened entrance way to one of the escape capsules and urged him inside. He held back a few seconds . . . I suppose, from his experience of getting blown out into space, he had *learned* that not much positive came from walking through external-leading doorways. But he did as I suggested.

No time to waste, I snapped the capsule door shut behind him.

Then turned to my own capsule.

If this didn't work, then I had no idea what I would do next.

Perhaps I would commandeer this cruiser, go get some pirate paperwork done and open my own line of retirement voyages . . . from what I hear, it can be a real nice earner.

Maybe it's time for *me* to think about retirement . . .

I waited for the precise moment I'd set back on the bridge.

When the cruiser would be passing right over the *Nava*.

I looked to the screen for the escape capsule, closed one eye, judging the coordinates readout, and then, finally, feeling the time was right, squeezed the launching trigger.

I watched on as the escape capsule shot free from its socket, and fired on down at the *Nava*. For a horribly unpleasant moment, I had visions of the capsule acting as a missile and smashing a hole right through my beloved . . . it wasn't my plan to kill Ellie.

That wouldn't help my cause any.

And I'd lose my Dear One at the same time.

As I eyed the escape capsule closing on the *Nava's* hull, I reached up and tapped away at the remote controls. I watched through the hatch as a beam shot out from the capsule, tethering the *Nava*, catching it smartly. And then, neatly, rumbling along in the *Nava's* wake. Although I hadn't *truly* doubted myself, I couldn't help but give a fist-pump . . . and I hoped there was no longer any functional surveillance system to catch that particular melodramatic, Hollywood-inspired moment.

I returned to the controls of the bridge, and, with a heavy

heart, plugged back the engines, reversing the throttle. Allowing the *Nava* to sprint on out ahead of the cruiser.

I held my breath—*literally*—wondering what might occur next.

The way I saw it, there were only two possibilities:

One, Ellie would fire on harder still, hoping to shake the capsule.

It was my hope that she believed *I* was inside it.

... And that Mr Trench Coat wouldn't be far behind.

The second possibility ...

A blinking light caught my attention.

I turned in its direction.

Proximity alarm.

I turned quickly.

My mind flurried.

Before I had any time to think, I saw an escape capsule fly right in front of the nose of the cruiser. It spun around and around, missing the shell of the ship by a hair or two. As I watched it pirouette on into the depth of space in the opposite direction from the *Nava*, I realised it was one of the *Nava's* escape capsules.

Ellie had realised my ploy.

She had decided to cut and run ... to simply get as far away from the scene as she could.

I wondered if it was a good or bad thing.

Then the rest of my plan sunk into my mind.

As *if* it was how I'd planned it all along.

Running—yeah, I *know!*—I reached the escape capsules another time, and, working far faster than I had with Mr Trench Coat, I clambered into the other one I had initialised.

Aimed it at the *Nava*.

I threw myself in through the porthole, and then slammed it shut behind.

I hardly had a second to get my thoughts straight before I felt myself being blasted free from the cruiser, firing directly for the hull of the *Nava*.

My head spun as the capsule rotated.

But my aim was true.

At the right moment, I squeezed the trigger.

Watched the laser beam fire out.

Seize hold of the *Nava*.

Draw me in beside Mr Trench Coat.

I eased my own escape capsule up alongside the starboard door of the *Nava*, and then slunk on up against it. I was inside, sat in my captain's chair, before I could even catch my breath.

With no time to relax, I turned my attention to Mr Trench Coat, still hanging off the side of the *Nava* like some kind of extra-terrestrial limpet in his own escape capsule.

Using the external shields—no doubt a detail that Ellie missed, if she ever did *really* want to get shot of that escape capsule; no matter who was in it—I maneuvered Mr Trench Coat's capsule about, and then, using the net force, generated a launch velocity.

My thumb hovered over the red release button for a satisfying few heartbeats before I allowed myself the pleasure of bringing it down. I watched on through the view screen as the capsule soared apart from the *Nava*, and off into the blackness of space . . . on the exact same trajectory as Ellie's escape capsule . . . the one which she had *purloined* from the *Nava*.

As I lay back in my captain's chair, propped my ever-so-tired ankles up onto the control board and allowed a well-earned and eager sleep to overcome me, I made a mental note to invoice Ellie for that escape capsule if we ever ended up bumping into one another again.

Yeah, right, like *that* was ever going to happen.

I supposed having avoided gaining a permanent travelling companion was payment enough for this particular job. Because no matter how much a smuggler might wish it to be so, not everything worthwhile can be purchased with credits.

LAPLAND-18

1

I SET THE *NAVA* DOWN in the terminal of Lapland-18, donned my snow gear, which, really, is just a fancy name for this nice, ersatz wool-lined leather jacket I picked up some place.

Quite possibly when I wasn't completely sober.

But I was glad for it then, because the moment that I stepped out of the terminal, I found myself locked in the middle of a snowstorm.

Now, anybody who's anybody about this universe of ours knows the deal with terraforming: simply put, we—*humans*—can do just about any damn thing we please with any planet we happen to grace with our presence.

Any climate we'd like.

And everybody—in the Lapland System—chose to go with full-out winter.

All year round.

See what I'm saying about nutters?

I yanked the collar of my jacket up to cover the fleshiest part of my neck, not wanting to find myself on the losing end of a cold this early in a job.

I don't think much to the Lapland System. Far as my thinking goes, any sort of a system that decides to dedicate itself to just one good, or service—*whatever*—is cruising for a bruising.

If you get what I mean.

The Lapland System, well, it dedicates itself solely to Christmas. Yeah, yeah; I know, all things Christmas ain't too shabby . . . I bet that's the riposte, right?

If you need some tinsel, or a pine tree, or a genetically modified reindeer that won't charge you, or shit in your living room, then you've got yourself a one-stop shop.

That's what Lapland's for.

Maybe, as a space smuggler, I'm so used to doing a little here, a little there, having a whole hoard of clients, that I could just never possibly see myself putting all my eggs in one basket and just *hoping* it'll be viable several years—*decades*—into the future.

Yeah, me and long-term thinking . . . go figure.

Guess my bigger beef with the place goes a little beyond my own personal business principles. It's more to do with the people.

Hell, let's not beat about the bush here, it's *always* about the people.

Out in this well-colonised universe of ours, there's just about a place for any James or Kelly.

Some place that they'll find to call 'home.'

One thing that I've got it in for with the Lapland System is the fact that there're people that're just *happy* to sit about all year working on Christmas *shit*.

I mean, doesn't that seem somewhat detached from the real world?

Yeah, thought so . . .

But my thinking really meant nothing at that point since my current job involved me hopping on over to the Lapland System to go pick up some pine trees for this rich family two systems over. Guess with all the festivities going on they didn't have some rat-ass servant going spare that they could chuck this particular menial task to. That's where *I* came in. Guess that was maybe the best part of the whole thing, that I wasn't going to be doing nothing illegal—not even anything borderline *illicit*. For Christmas's sake. Just as if some nobleman, back on Earth, many centuries ago, had called out to some ragamuffin hanging about the street, flipped him a shilling and told him to go grab him a turkey on Christmas Day . . . think there's some story I'm taking that from.

I scanned the street outside the terminal for any sign of public transportation, and—who would've thought it?—this sleigh ploughed on out from the flurrying snow, one of those golden-shining lanterns hanging from its runners; a pair of genetically modified reindeer lugging the thing along. As the sleigh drew up to me, I saw, sitting up there, on the driver's seat, there was a man dressed in a Father Christmas costume. I could see nothing of his face for his hood, but I could just about *feel* the jolliness oozing right out of him.

Instantly, I felt myself drowning in a whole bunch of smells encompassing the whole yuletide spectrum: Christmas pudding, chocolate log, roast turkey . . . and I have to admit that it got me to feeling just a mite hungry. And when I get hungry, I *really* get hungry.

My stomach quivered.

Wanting to get something inside my portly frame.

But my logical mind, thankfully, won out that particular battle.

I gazed up at this impromptu Father Christmas, and said, "Looking for some Christmas trees, you got any?"

The Father Christmas tightened his hold on the reins, and looked out into the snow storm, which, I swear, just swilled around and around on some infinite loop.

Damn terraforming.

"Yup, think I could fix you up, partner."

'Partner'?

I thought about picking up on that particular form of address, but decided to let it slide. Anybody who refers to me as anything else other than 'Captain' or 'Captain Wright' gets on my nerves just a tad. Guess that's the thing about being a professional. It irks you when you don't get the respect you surely deserve.

"How much?" I asked.

The Father Christmas named a—not-unreasonable—fee in Fritten Credits and I clambered on up into the carriage which sat on the back of the sleigh.

And we headed off.

Into the never-ending snowstorm.

2

I HAVE TO ADMIT, to begin with, I found something slightly enjoyable about my sleigh ride.

It kinda conformed with all my greatest expectations.

Back on my home planet—back on Arkle Four—snow'd only been this distant thing which we saw on TV, or heard about from off-planet pilots, travellers.

Since my childhood, though, I'd had more than my fair share of snow experiences and to say that I wasn't crying out for another one would've been putting it mildly.

But I had a job to do.

Still, a sleigh ride.

Not too shabby for a working man.

Things only became somewhat rocky when the Father Christmas pulled up the sleigh to the side of the road, and some hapless individual hopped in.

This particular hapless individual turned out to be a lady—maybe in her late forties, early fifties—with wild, untameable, wiry black hair which stuck up all about her scalp like some kind of scouring pad. She had her arms full of all these elaborately wrapped gifts. All of them shiny and with neat bows tied on top. She smelled, for some reason, of roasted almonds.

That made my mouth salivate just a touch.

Like I said, I was getting hungry.

With an unexpected *jerk*, the Father Christmas-slash-sleigh driver shunted us back off on our way. Leaving me and the woman with some sort of conversation to get on with.

I sort of looked her over out the corner of my eye, noting how, every ten seconds or so, she would busy herself with one of the packages—with some aspect of the packaging.

It might be flattening out a bit of paper, or tying one of the ribbons a little tighter, but she was constantly on the move. Apparently unable to keep herself still.

Even though it's against the smugglers' code, or, at least, against my code, I decided that I'd give small talk a go.

Just like I'd seen it done in films, I cleared my throat.

That brought her attention away from her highly-strung manipulations of the packages she gathered about herself, and onto me.

"Ma'am," I said, nodding my head.

Her dormouse-like eyes all skittered about mine. "Sir?"

"You, uh," I said, eyeing the packages, "off to go exchange gifts, or some such?"

She gave me a steely gaze. "No," she said, her tone flat and almost like she was scolding a child, "I'm off to take these down to the delivery depot. Pre-arranged."

"Ah, I see."

The woman's lips parted slightly as if she might say something more. But, instead, she turned her attention back out the frosted window, to the perpetually falling snow.

After the sleigh had rocked on for another ten minutes, and the woman had had made no gesture that she was about to alight, I tried out some more of that small talk.

"Your business don't have a delivery service of its own? Gotta shift about town in one of these sleighs to deliver every last package?"

The woman sniffed. She didn't look away from the window. "I'm a sole proprietor."

I just sort of notched my head back and latched my lips apart in understanding.

Not that she so much as looked at me.

Five minutes later, the lady shifted on out of the sleigh and, piling her packages, she ventured back on out into the storm. Apparently having arrived at her destination.

Like I said, people from the Lapland System are weird.

No way around it.

3

THE FATHER CHRISTMAS drove the sleigh on for what felt like another quarter of an hour before bringing it to a halt. I heard his rugged voice through the thick ersatz wood of the carriage.

"End o' the line!"

Not wanting to stay on Lapland-18 any longer than I absolutely had to, I shifted my hefty arse off over the cushions of the carriage, and out into the street.

When I got out, I paid the Father Christmas his credits, and then set off in the direction he indicated for me. I slouched on for a good five minutes, burning off who knows how many calories. I knew I had reached my destination when I spotted the endless pine trees all sprouting up from the snowed-over landscape. Those little bursts of green in an otherwise featureless wasteland.

At least for me this was a wasteland.

As I wandered on in through the chain-link fence to the place, one thing that I couldn't quite set straight was why they'd set up this forest so far out of town. I soon got my answer to that one, though, when I spotted, off in the distance, the flare of a rocket launching itself up into space.

It appeared that they had their own space station out here.

The company was called—pretty unimaginatively, in my opinion—*Pine Corp*, and its logo pretty much consisted of a cartoon pine tree with a snowy background.

Maybe it was meant to be somewhat kitsch, or whatever.

To me, though, it just looked like shit.

This soulless employee sat at a sad-looking pine desk and tapped away lifelessly at a touchscreen. I did my old throat-clearing trick once more, and his attention snapped onto me.

I say 'snapped,' but maybe 'turned at a glacial pace' is a better approximation..

The kid wore a light-blue suit which had several muddy stains that he—or whoever washed his clothes—hadn't quite ever managed to get out. He most definitely had all the aspects of the second-generation Laplander. Parents had probably thought that it might be 'novel' for them to move into a system where it was Christmas every day. And they had, no doubt, enjoyed it so much that they'd decided to reproduce. To sprog out this offspring sitting before me.

And now he had had to suffer this merriment.

Every. Day. Of. His. Life.

Could I blame him for looking all slouchy and uninterested?

Perhaps not . . .

"Looking for some trees," I said. "Special order."

I gave him the name of my client—this rich family—and the kid jabbed through a whole bunch of options on his screen. He snorted hard, drawing some—*surely*—hard flecks of phlegm right down his throat. He scratched his slightly stubbly throat, coughed, and then lugged himself up out of his chair with no end of grief. He led me along a corridor and out to the trees.

Although I found myself just a touch awed by the sight, I couldn't help noticing that the kid looked nowhere but to the snow right before his feet. The kid's whole aspect was so dejected that I almost missed his words drifting back at me over his shoulder. "Private courier, huh?"

"What?"

The kid glanced round at me for precisely *one* micro second. "Them clients of yours too good for our standard shipping service?"

"Huh? Oh, yeah, I guess so."

I've never really subscribed to that whole business of having to respect your clients—the one's that're handing you the dough. It's not like they're going to hear what you've said about them. Not unless they've got somebody spying on you. Anyway, as a rule of thumb, I never really go out of my way to badmouth them, but if somebody's got some fairly strong views on my clients, I don't see it as my task to steer them right either.

The kid rolled his shoulders in a way which suggested to me that he'd spent a good deal of time slouched up at that desk before I'd disturbed him.

With all this walking, I felt like the pounds were melting off me. "You ain't got any other way of getting to trees—a faster way?"

"Nah. Pa's got all the drones shifting stuff. Busy at this time of year. Got half of Fritten on Christmas."

I just nodded back to him, in a way that I hoped he'd interpret as understanding.

When a large portion of the biggest human-colonised system in the universe celebrates Christmas, it really *celebrates* Christmas. I guessed that all the planets in the Lapland System were working overtime for Fritten. And I could sort of empathise a little more with the kid that some clients just wouldn't take the standard shipping service, the service that just about everybody else in the universe seemed perfectly content to utilise. Still, arseholes are a fact of life.

No shaking them, I guess.

Finally, the kid brought me before this row of what looked like *quite nice* trees.

There was half a dozen of them.

All bundled together.

Apparently pre-selected and planted here, judging by the recently disturbed mounds of dirt beneath them.

"This them?" I said, to probably no end whatsoever.

"Uh-huh," the kid said, and then, from down at his belt, he removed an electro cutter, and set himself to work.

Before long, he'd got all the trees lying down in the fluffy, white snow.

Replacing the electro cutter on his belt, he glanced over me and said, in a bored voice, "Just how exactly were you planning on carting these trees away?"

"Uh," I said, now seeing this problem for myself. "Dunno."

"Gonna cost a good deal to have a private sleigh come on up here to lug them along. Public sleigh service won't take on this sort of a load. More than their job's worth."

"How much is a 'good deal'?" I asked.

He gave me a number that made me very unhappy. It would work out to be more than half of the fee I was getting to do this shitty job in the first place.

I was thinking of simply cutting my losses when the kid reached up and scratched his throat. Doing so caused his stubble to make a rasping sound. "Wanna make a deal?"

"What'd you mean?"

The kid looked at me with thoroughly dead eyes. He pressed his lips together tightly so that all the blood left them, and then said, in a voice devoid of all emotion, "I fucking hate snow. Please, I beg you, take me away from here."

4

ANOTHER SLEIGH RIDE LATER, and I found myself back at the old familiar controls of the *Nava*. And I had to admit that I was feeling pretty damn pleased with myself.

I'd managed to stop myself from losing a whole shit ton of money and it looked like I'd made a friend in the process too . . . who says that business and friendship never mix?

I guess the same person that thinks that a space smuggler never gets lonely.

As per the kid's instructions, I chugged the *Nava* all the way along to the coordinates he had indicated, and there I found the trees all lying there in the snow.

The kid himself, despite his apparent desperation to get away from Lapland-18, seemed pretty much as deadpan as before. He stood there nonchalant with his hands stuffed into the pockets of his overalls. I wondered if he really knew what he was doing . . . or if he was acting on some sort of a whim. I was just here to do a job. I wasn't here to give people life coaching . . . no matter how useful I might be at providing that sort of a service . . .

I dialled him up on my comms and—between the two of us—we finally got the trees all loaded up into the hold of the *Nava*. After we'd got that all done, and with the two of us sweating out enough to sure cause a minor environmental disaster within the artificial atmosphere of Lapland-18, we stood about in the hold, the ramp down, and with the both of us looking at the snow.

The kid didn't give me so much as a smile. He just stood about like normal. Then he stared back at me. "So, the deal stands?"

I looked him in the eye and I saw something there. I wouldn't like to speculate too much, all I can say is that there was *something* . . . something which set some sort of an alarm system—an advanced-warning, whatever you might want to call it—jangling about the thick chamber of my skull.

It wasn't right.

Something about this whole setup wasn't right.

I reached down for my side and—*surprise, surprise*—I'd gone and left my space blaster in the cockpit of the *Nava*. If I had a credit for every time I managed to leave my blaster behind somewhere when I needed it fairly urgently, well . . . I wouldn't be doing space smuggling no more, that's for certain.

Was it the kid's eyes?

How they were glowing a slight shade of red?

Was that it?

. . . No, that wasn't it at all.

When I finally caught onto it, I was just in time to see the overalls busting at the seams, and the antlers coming bursting on out of the kid's skull. They broke through the skin like fledgling branches and soon twisted around themselves, seeming to become thicker as they did so. Then the boy's legs became all stumpy, until they resembled more hind legs than legs . . . well, I say 'resembled' but the truth of the thing was that they really *were* a reindeer's legs. And now the boy had been replaced by a kind of reindeer.

No, an *actual* reindeer.

And one with a bright-red, *glowing* nose.

Rudolph?

I thought quickly, and I bashed my fist against the button on the wall of the loading bay. Slowly—*too slowly!*—I heard the mechanism grind into action, the ramp closing itself shut, and blocking out Lapland-18.

The boy-slash-reindeer launched himself at me.

I judged it just right.

The boy-slash-reindeer stood tottering right on the edge of the ramp.

Would he fall into the loading bay?

Or tumble into the snowdrift outside?

Though I may be thick-skulled, I do have a decent survival instinct. I barrelled forwards and struck the boy-slash-reindeer with the very best shoulder charge I could muster.

The boy-slash-reindeer tumbled on out of the landing bay.

Landed with a *whoomph!* in the snow dune outside.

The landing bay ramp shut with a satisfying—but not particularly dramatic—*clunk*.

I put my legs into motion just as quickly as I could, and I bundled on along the corridor of the *Nava*, all the way back to the cockpit where I set the take-off boosters to work.

This was one time when I could really do with things going smoothly.

And thankfully they did.

As I rose up off the sad face of Lapland-18, I gazed down through the cockpit window and to the boy-slash-reindeer lying there in the snow dune, and looking somewhat beleaguered.

It wasn't till I punctured the atmosphere that I allowed myself a real smile.

I squeezed tight to the thrusters, and shot right out into Big Black.

Safe.

Whatever that meant.

And with credits in hand.

It wasn't such a bad life.

A new lesson learned, too.

Perhaps those genetically modified reindeers weren't quite the marvellous things I had always thought them to be.

THE LEWD LARKHOUSE

1

IF I HAD to pick one of all the nuts in the whole universe to be the very worst then I really couldn't see much past the drug nut. Oh, sure, there's the religious nut, the political nut, the scientific nut can be a particularly tricky one to shift. But at least them types all tend to follow some specific megalomaniacal creed, some sort of unifying trend. The drug nut, though, well, the simple truth of the thing is that there *is* no trend.

They just gotta get their fix and that's all there is to it.

Now, maybe there'd be a fresh talker, or some, who'd chew into me about my taste for the odd moiser here and there. And, yes, guilty I'd have to admit that near enough half the time I'm all saturated with alcohol up to my eardrums. Is that a drug? Sure. But does that get in the way of me making an honest buck here and there? Not usually . . . at least not that I've noticed. Oh I bet that it's made a job a mite trickier here and there, but to have moiser actually get *right* in the way of me doing what a space smuggler's gotta get done . . . not so much.

I was running low of something, that was for sure, clsc the *Nava*—that's my beloved spaceship—wouldn't have been whining at me like a bitch in heat. If there's one thing in the whole world that I simply *can't* ignore it's when my ship gets to feeling in some sort of pain.

Guess it might be comparable to what a mother might feel for a sick child or some such.

When I tapped out on my navigational screens, I found that

there was a planet nearby—this place known as Tal-19, which meant that it was right towards the end of its system. There's always issues with outer planets. Just something about being a long way from the star seems to get into the water . . . maybe some scientist nut might be able to better explain it.

I did a quick scan to see if I could give the Tal System a miss, but no dice.

I needed to bed down here right now.

The first thing that sparked some sort of a warning signal inside of my space smuggler brain was the fact that when I called up video comms I just got stuck with this whole screen load of fuzz. I mean, like, *real* fuzz. I actually stared at that whole mess of distortion for several seconds trying to make some sort of sense of it.

But, no matter what I did, I couldn't bring it clear.

So I switched to audio.

"Hey, down there," I said into the comms, "Anybody feel like giving me some clearance?"

I sat back in my chair, feeling the springs all coil up beneath my substantial weight, and I watched the screen for a response. I've been to so many places within the universe that I've come across abandoned terminals before—*ghost* terminals I guess you'd call them—now, I wasn't totally convinced that this was one of them places, but I was certainly catching that drift. And it wasn't just the *Nava* that was barking out at me, my stomach too was doing a few leaps. I'd got through most of my backup rations in the past few hours and really needed to do some stocking up. If these reprobates weren't going to get back to me so much as to give me clearance to pound on down to their shitstain of a planet . . . well, I might just be fit to burst . . . that or I'd lose a few kilos in the process.

Something babbled through the comms system. Some audio that I had no chance at all at comprehending. So I dished out just what I always dish out in them circumstances.

"Huh?" I said.

There was some distortion on the line—I mean some *more* distortion seeing as the whole of the audio feed seemed to be a base level of distortion—and then I heard a vague, ". . . Ship . . . ?"

I breathed in hard at the sulphur-smelling air of the *Nava* and wondered if it was maybe the cooling systems, or ventilation, that'd got all bummed out.

Wasn't worth stressing about it till I got an expert to take a look.

Because, even though I spend a pretty substantial amount of time inside of the *Nava*, I really haven't spent any time at all trying to unravel its mysteries . . . like the basics of how anything —*anything at all*—works.

"Yeah," I said into the comms, "a spaceship looking to land— that okay with you fellas?"

Though the distortion continued to spray out of the comms, I thought I heard a little bit of idiotic laughter. I held still, told myself not to freak out or anything, not to get all angry and tell whoever was down there having a mighty good time to pull them- selves together.

"I got permission, or not?" I said.

A long wave of static—what might've been more laughter—and then, finally, ". . . 'kay."

I guessed that was the best I was going to get from them so I flipped the switch that does all the complicated landing stuff, and I was on my way.

2

NOW, usually, at any self-respecting terminal, there's a whole manner of *stuff* buzzing about the place. You know, all them drones, or bots just cramming about all the parked ships: servicing this, or that. And I had sort of been banking on one of them drones or bots—whichever was cheaper—fixing up the *Nava*.

Yeah, there was none of that.

There weren't even many other ships.

In fact, even with my brain as addled with moiser as it was—as per usual—I could only count the one. And this one looked somewhat unfit for flying, which was to say that it seemed in approximately a hundred or so pieces.

I set the *Nava* to rest on my assigned landing pad and then I lugged myself up off my lardy bottom. I banked out of the *Nava*—taking extreme care to engage the security systems—and then I shucked on into the terminal itself.

It took a good five minutes' walking.

That's another thing about self-respecting terminals, they don't *allow* you to *walk* anywhere. Still, I tried to tell myself that there might be a strike on, or that I might've taken a wrong turn and ended up in the old—abandoned—terminal.

There was nobody at immigration controls. There was a sign there, but the bot that did the checking was all clunked out even when I scanned my bios. It didn't make so much as a peep as I stepped through the disengaged force field door to the terminal proper: the departures lounge.

When I looked out among all the seats—most of them with

foam sticking out from the upholstery—I couldn't help wondering if I was going to see a cute little bundle of tumbleweed come rolling on into the scene.

There was nobody here.

Like, nobody at all.

I turned about, tried to work out what might've happened.

There *had* been voices on the other end of the comms, so I at least knew that there *was* somebody hanging about the terminal. The trick of the thing now would be to actually track them down.

I spotted the sign soon enough, the one that read *Staff Only* and I supposed that it would be a start.

3

NO ESCALATOR, no lift, nothing like that.

Just plain, old stairs.

Every five steps, or so, I had to pause to hoik my trousers back up over the crack of my bum. Only after I'd gone through that motion for about the dozenth time did I decide it really wasn't worth the hassle. It wasn't like there was anybody about here to tell me any different. In many ways, it was just like being back on the *Nava* all over again.

I found my way to the top of the staircase, and I glanced along all the doors there, pausing ever so briefly at each one to read the label.

I eventually found Traffic Control right at the end of the corridor.

The door wasn't locked.

In fact, the door was half open.

"Knock, knock," I said, as I eased myself in around the side of it.

As I stood in the doorway, I found myself staring right back at a pair of kids no older than fifteen years old. The two of them looked surprised to see me there, and their eyes were all wild and their hair stood on end as if they'd seen a ghost or something.

I have to admit that I relished striking fear into this pair of boys just for a few moments. There's something very animal about being able to inspire fear in other human beings.

"Uh," I said, "either of you two boys know where a good gentleman smuggler can find a fix for his ship?"

The boys just continued on staring at me with them bulbous eyes of theirs. The two of them had their mouths just a little propped open as if their brains were about to slip and slide right out past their teeth.

"Hello?" I said, frowning as I waited for my response.

The boys just kept on staring.

Finally, after what must've been about ten seconds or more, one of the boys moved his lips just a touch. I guessed that he was the brains of the two. ". . . Ship?" he said.

I looked to that boy and then to the other. "Yeah?" I said. "I've got a *ship*. A *ship* that needs some fixing, so if you'd be so kind as to send me off in the direction of senior management then I'll be on my way."

The boys didn't reply.

I sighed long and hard.

Because, even then, I could see just what was afoot.

I stepped over to them, waved my hand in front of their stony gazes.

No response.

Pupils dilated.

Mouths ajar.

I sighed again. "All right," I said, "where'd you boys get hold of it?"

"Huh?" the boy who'd spoken before said.

"The stuff—whatever you've drugged yourselves up with."

The boy seemed to absorb what I was saying . . . but there's a pretty big difference between *absorbing* something and *understanding* it.

I looked to the two boys, hoping to find a cue, and that was when I saw it.

Lying on the control panel of the Traffic board.

An auto applicator.

Since neither of the boys seemed to be much in the mood to stop me, I reached past them and grabbed a hold of it. I looked at the glass chamber in the centre, saw that there was the remains of a lime-green liquid within. I could see that the needle of the applicator still had a smudge of blood on it . . . I guessed that these two'd just gone and used the same applicator.

Like I said, a drug nut's gonna be a drug nut.

"Where," I started, holding the applicator up, "did you get this?"

Both the boys continued to stare me down and I knew a lost cause when I saw one, so I trudged on out of Traffic Control shaking my head and wondering just how I was going to get my ship all fixed up. As I stood in the doorway, ready to leave, to work out just where everybody else had got to, one of the boys spoke.

"Uh, Mister?"

I was in such a pissy mood by then that I snarled, "Captain," in reply.

This seemed to stump the poor kid—he just didn't seem capable of meeting the frayed ends. It was all double-dutch to him.

"The place," the boy said, obviously taking great care with all the words he spoke as if—were he to speak them wrong—they might set a thermonuke pounding. "Place we go's called . . ." but the boy trailed off.

Thankfully, though, Boy Genius had his silent-till-then companion to pick up the slack.

"Lark ... *house*," he finally got out.

"Huh?" I said. "The 'Larkhouse?'"

Both boys gave me that same glassy stare of theirs and I guessed that was the best I was going to get from them, and so I shucked out to check out the rest of Tal-19—this so-called planet.

4

I LEARNED pretty soon that it seemed like dust had eaten up just about everything.

It was this bright red dust, and it swept about all over the roads, and billowed up in clouds, and it rained down too.

From what I could tell, there was a dust storm blowing in. Through the clouds of dust, I could just about make out shapes of buildings. The light from the star—from Tal—was a bright yellow and in a certain way of looking at the dust, it made it seem almost green.

I stomped across the street, away from the terminal, and into the next building along.

As I stood before it, I glanced up and took in the name.

Hal's Accounts

I breathed in the thick dust on the air and then, feeling an especially fierce gust of dust brewing up behind me, I stepped through the automated doors.

Strangely, *Hal's Accounts* seemed to be way better held together than the terminal. In fact, I got the impression that it was better *used* than the terminal. Standing inside the place, looking about, I noticed that it was *clean* . . . that there was a cashiers' window . . . that, on the other side of the glass, there was *people*.

Finally, I was going to get some answers.

There was no line and one of the attendants saw to me right away. The only problem of the thing was contending with the speaker in the glass. The accent here on Tal I found somewhat difficult to understand right away.

But, then again, I *had* had a few moisers on the journey over.

The woman I spoke to behind the glass wore a prim, laser-blue suit . . . though I knew that it was just the colour scheme of the bank, I couldn't help wondering if that exact tone hadn't been picked out so that it might match her eyes.

And I half thought about commenting on it.

Only the reminder of the howls of the *Nava* stopped me.

Some things are too important to put off for another second longer.

We got through the preliminaries, and then I asked, "You heard of a place where I can get my ship all fixed up?"

The woman pursed her lips. She furrowed her brow. Though she'd been totally lucid till that moment I'd asked *that* question, she now seemed to slip into a daze . . . a daze reminiscent to them kids back at the terminal. ". . . 'Ship?'" she said.

I pushed back the urge to sigh again, telling myself that I needed to be civil if I was to obtain the help I needed. "Yeah," I said. "I need some repairs for my ship"—I jerked my thumb over my shoulder in the direction of where I'd just come—"parked up there, in the *terminal*."

"'Terminal?'" she said.

"There an echo in here?" I replied, and looked to the two other attendants all standing about behind the glass, and the two of them both gawping as much as the woman seeing to me.

"Sir," the lady said, "I simply don't know what you're talking about."

I thought about getting down to basics, to literally going through the whole evolution of space travel. But, I guessed, if she wanted to put some effort into researching the thing then she could do so . . . not my responsibility to educate the dunces of the world, that's for sure.

I recalled what them two boys had said to me back at the terminal, when I'd seen that drug they'd been shooting each other up with. How they'd said that . . . *thing* . . . it struck me then and I asked the lady, flat-out, "You know any place called the Larkhouse?"

The lady remained still for a couple of moments, and then she glanced to the other attendants. I held my breath, waiting for my answer. And then, without any further warning, the automated metal guard rolled down on the other side of the glass. Shuttered me off from the attendants there right away.

On instinct, I reached down to my belt, for my blaster.

I felt the substantial rubber grip.

Gave it a squeeze as if it was my favourite teddy.

I expected some sort of kill bots, or some bomber drones, to come bursting on in through the doors to the bank. But nothing came. Nothing happened. All the same, I slipped my blaster out of its holster and I gripped it tight.

There's nothing much like it to inspire confidence in a man— or a woman for that matter—than a space blaster in hand, and the knowledge that the safety is flipped off.

Seeing as I was, apparently, no longer welcome at the bank, I stepped on out.

Back into the dust storm.

THOUGH I DID pass a few other businesses on Tal—complete with other people—I chose to give them a fairly wide berth. There didn't seem to be much point to upsetting these people. They clearly didn't want to be told about spaceships, or terminals, or asked about the Larkhouse, for that matter.

I went past places called *Adam's Bun Shop, Cyndi's Cuts* and *Tyson's Stitches.*

I very much got a whole home-grown vibe off Tal-19, though I can't say that I really found any aspect of it comforting at all.

I reached this tiny little park—with all this cute greenery, shielded from the raging dust by a semi-translucent, force field bubble. It was nice to breathe in some fresh air for a change . . . I mean fresh air untouched by dust, or whatever that stuff was. I was thinking about whether I maybe should've stopped by at *Adam's Buns* . . . or whatever the place'd been called . . . and that was how my mind got all stuck on sugary tastes in an almost feverish way.

Inside the park, the air was cool against my skin and this fountain made a gentle *tinkle* as it spilled water all over itself.

I caught sight of a pair of women. The women seemed to be in about their sixties, and probably nothing would've drawn my attention to them except for the fact that the two of them, sat on a bench beside one another, were near enough losing their breakfast with laughter about something or other.

I soon saw the explanation.

A pair of them auto-applicators, like I'd seen back at the terminal, that them boys had been using, lay at their feet. The same glass chambers with the lime-green liquid all smudged on the inside. I bided my time, stayed on the periphery and wondered if they might be dangerous. Then I told myself that I was a grown man—a grown man with a *blaster*—so I should just grow a pair.

I headed up to the women, addressed them as politely as I could manage, and asked them about the Larkhouse.

The two of them, just like the boys at the terminal had done, looked at me with them great bulbous eyes. I thought that I was going to find myself on the receiving end of something far more unpleasant than the sharp end of an umbrella when one of them seemed to have a lucid moment and said, "Lark . . . Larkhouse," and then shakily pointed past me, over my shoulder, and up the hill that ran away from the park.

When I followed just where she indicated, I near enough slapped my cheeks.

I mean, the place on the hill was this dirty, great big mansion. It was a copper colour and it looked just about as ominous as all those horrific places you can find in films, and such.

All the same, I nodded to the ladies and then headed on out of the park.

And up the hill.

6

NOW, I've never been a great walker, and right then I have to admit that I was struggling after, oh, maybe ten paces or so. I can just about handle flat when I have to, but when the vertical dimension gets added into the mix, that's when I really begin to have a struggle on my hands. I had a struggle on my hands right then.

I felt the hot tug at the backs of my calves and tried to put it out of my mind. I could feel the sweat leaking down my forehead, those hot—*too hot*—salty beads snaking their way all over my face. The gentle odour of salt everywhere. I could hear my panting, too, and that didn't help me feel any manlier about the whole deal.

I reached into my pocket hoping that I might find some sort of sustenance within.

No luck.

I just had to keep climbing.

And so I did, right the way to the top.

When I reached the mansion, I expected there to be some notional security, but there wasn't anything at all. Just a big pair of *ersatz* oak doors with no lock on them. I pushed on through and into the place that'd been told to me was the Larkhouse.

INSIDE, the place stank a little of damp and old, muddy boots. Breathing it was a little like sniffing a wet dog arse-first. The place wasn't all that well heated, either. I could feel a wicked draught spilling all about my feet, bringing my skin up in welts. My mouth tasted a little of blood on account of the striding up the hill.

I glanced about the interior of the place, over the black-and-white tiles—unpolished—and then, seeing that there wasn't much else for me to do, I called out.

"*He*-llo!"

My own words echoed back at me.

I don't rightly know just what I was expecting, if I was thinking that I was going to drive out another drug nut from some nook or cranny of the place, somebody just about as coherent as Tweedledee and Tweedledum back at the terminal.

But that wasn't what happened at all.

Because, from out of the shadows of one of the side passages of the hall, this boxy little man emerged. He wore a white coat and had a pair of round-framed spectacles perched on the bridge of his nose.

I tried—*I really did*—not to sigh at all, but I couldn't help it.

Scientists, really, especially *rogue* scientists, cooped up in some backwater of the universe, are perhaps the very worst of them all.

The scientist blinked at me a couple dozen of times, looked a little unsure about the whole deal, and then broke into an unconvincing smile. "Hello there," he said, approaching me.

I reached down for my belt, for my blaster there. I drew it out. "You hold it," I said. "Don't you take another step."

The scientist did as I said.

"Hands where I can see 'em."

Again, he did as I asked.

I held still, the blaster pointing at him. "What the hell have you got going on this here planet, then, what's this stuff you're serving up to these people?"

The scientist frowned a little. "You're . . . you're from off-planet?"

"Seems so, Frankenstein."

"But, I . . . *how?*"

Though those kids had been a fair pair of drug nuts, I knew that I was better off not mentioning them. They really hadn't done all that much wrong—nothing so that they might deserve some 'punishment' from this character.

"Oh, I'm a space smuggler—we have our ways when we need to get parked for repairs."

"'Repairs?'" the scientist repeated at me, and, just for a second, I wondered if he was going to go all ogle-eyed like the rest of the planet upon hearing about terminals, space travel, etcetera. But then he added, "Your ship is damaged?"

"Why else you think I parked up on this shit-stain of a planet?"

The scientist blinked a couple of times at my profanity, though I've never been able to work out why scientists—as a race—are so down on frank-speak.

Guess you've gotta be one to know one, and I've no intention of *ever* being one.

"I just want some repairs," I said. "Then I'll shift on off this place."

The scientist cracked a smile at this, though I couldn't quite understand why.

I mean, it's not like having a blaster pointed right at you inspires much in the way of a warm tickle in the gut.

The scientist shook his head a couple of times. "I never thought . . . *didn't* think that . . . well, that anybody would manage to land here."

"Yeah? Well I *did*."

The scientist breathed in deeply. His shoulders rolled upwards with the action. I knew this next part by heart. I know just how much scientists driven mad with power like to show off their 'genius' to individuals outside their little rat mazes . . . and this little rat maze was known as Tal-19.

"Captain," the scientist said, and the only reason I allowed him to stay talking for so long was because he addressed me in the proper way, "You must be wondering why the people here—why *nobody* here—quite understands the whole concept of space travel."

Still keeping the blaster trained on the bastard, I said, "Yeah, that's half of it, no doubt, but the other half has more to do with those screw-brained people bobbing about in the gaps—you know, the ones that can't function?"

The scientist, still holding his hands up over his head, gave a slight nod. "Yes, Captain, please, allow me to explain."

"This gonna get me some repairs?" I asked.

He didn't answer the question, but I assumed it was because

he was so wrapped up in explaining his genius to me that he simply didn't feel he had time.

"Here, I wanted to create a serum—a *drug*—that might wipe a certain part of a person's brain, keep them from imagining, or being *able* to imagine, certain scenarios. The specific one that I wished to separate, as you've seen, is that ability to consider *leaving* the planet."

"And why in all hell would you want to do that?"

The scientist's eyes shone brightly for a moment, and then he said, "Because, Captain, I believe in the Sky Gods of Tal-19, ever since . . ."

I held up my hand. This nutter had ticked three out of four now, which was to say that he was a drug, scientist and religious nut.

To say that I'd had enough and wanted to get back to the usual of belting out into space in the hardy belly of the *Nava* was Understatement of the Year.

I wasn't all that into hearing this guy's political screeds.

I had no interest in ticking that fourth nutter box.

But, it seemed, the scientist had other ideas in mind.

And he managed to get speaking again before I had the chance to stop him with force.

". . . All I wanted was a utopia, some place where everybody could be happy, not have to *think* about space." He paused for a moment. "And, well, I suppose that you've seen for yourself how the serum has been a raging success, except for those rare cases where it turns the host's brain to something approaching jelly."

"Where's the antidote?" I asked.

"'Antidote?'" the scientist asked, and then grimaced a touch.

"Captain, there's no antidote, but if those taking the serum cease to take it then they'll eventually lose the block on their mind, the one which prevents them from imagining a world apart from Tal-19."

"Where'd you cook the stuff?"

At this, the scientist got a little het-up. His eyes got wider like I'd just said I was going to smother his firstborn in its cot.

"Captain?"

I squeezed the trigger of my blaster.

It blew off a huge chunk of the black-and-white tile at the scientist's toe.

It seemed to get his attention.

"This way," he said, his eyes several shades of panic.

8

THE SCIENTIST led me down a whole bunch of windy passages through his mansion.

I suppose I should've been a little more aware that he might have something nasty in mind for me. That he might be wanting to sort of, I don't know, have me fall into some pit or something that he had waiting for me.

But, sure enough, he led me right to the lab where he cooked up the stuff.

And, I realised, as we stood there, in the doorway, that he was just glad—like almost all scientists—to be able to show off his true genius to an outsider. More than likely, he had been waiting all his life for some off-planet stranger to land here so that he might detail out just how bright he truly was.

I made light work of the lab.

I might not be much in the way of an engineer—certainly no *mechanic* either—but I knew that if I blew up all the glass flasks, made as much of a mess of the stuff as I possibly could, that it would make things mighty difficult for my friend the scientist.

When I turned back to the scientist, I saw that he was in tears.

His megalomaniacal little paradise was in tatters now.

He hadn't banked on Arkle Wright doing the damage.

With that done, I picked out a nice little secure part of the mansion—a room with a lock—and I deposited the scientist within.

He didn't put up a fight at all.

He seemed to understand that the show was over.

That he had had his kicks for a while and now was the time for something approaching punishment.

I felt nothing except for relief for the people of Tal-19 when I turned the key to the lock of that room—I'd left him in what appeared to be a pantry so I knew that he was going to be just fine for surely the rest of his lifetime with all those cans.

And when I trod back on down the hill—going downhill was *way* easy thank goodness—I felt like something approaching a hero.

Oh, I know that heroes aren't *ever* supposed to actually feel like they are heroes, but I have to admit that I certainly felt like one right then.

I waited out the time, and, just as the scientist had confided in me after I'd locked him in the pantry, the people all seemed to snap back to life after a week of not taking their drug . . . or their 'serum,' as the scientist put it.

The terminal, soon enough, filled with the hustle and bustle of life, and all them people who'd been shanking about the planet jabbering this and that snapped back to their senses, and returned to being normal people once more.

The best thing about saving Tal-19 was that I got a mechanic to do some work on the *Nava,* and though I really should've asked for it to be done *pro bono,* what with me having saved them all from the scourge of *that* scientist, I knew it would be a tricky thing since I didn't really have any proof that I had freed them.

If the scientist here had intended Tal-19 to be a sort of religious sanctuary, then I actually felt like something approaching a saint when I handed over a healthy tip to the mechanic who got the work done on the *Nava*. He thanked me kindly and I just grinned back at him.

To tell the truth, nothing much beat sitting back at the controls of the *Nava* and blasting myself a long way away from Tal-19 . . . I guessed that I'd earned the feeling of escaping the scientist's clutches.

But, I had to admit, I was beginning to wonder if I should invest in one of those Basics Mechanics courses they give.

Just to be on the safe side.

Just so as not to end up in places like Tal-19.

PLANET OF MISERY

1

THERE AIN'T MUCH WORSE than somebody who always paints in black.

If you don't catch onto my meaning there then I'd be mighty worried that you could just be one of those people.

You know the kind, dontcha?

The ones who walk around, heads pointing to the ground, mumbling to themselves.

Yep, if you just picture that in your mind and take a picture you'd have a pretty good idea of just how Gunnaral-40 is.

Nobody really knows what gets all the people so depressed, and such, though I've heard of a few theories in the afterhours at *The Bitch's Leap*—my normal drinking hole out there on Horte-nine-6, which is really another sorry state of a planet, to tell the truth.

Maybe people on Gunnaral are all het up about the proximity of their nearest star—and how scientists down there seem to be constantly bleating on about how it's gonna go *pop!* any time of its choosing.

Yeah, that could be one explanation.

I mean, who likes to wake up every morning staring their own mortality in the eye first thing?

Suppose they could move away, only that the planet's so poor that the only real way out for any kid wanting to reach for the stars tends to be joining up with the FSA: the Fritten Space Authorities . . . doing just what I did to get out of my own pit of sludge, my own home planet: Arkle-4.

But those that stay behind—that's the majority of them—the ones who aren't fit for service with the FSA and can't either seem to get hold of a space-running job no how, they're the ones who go mooching about the planet with their heads bowed staring at the kinda shit-coloured dirt.

Yeah, I guess that no prospects and a *shit*-coloured planet is just about enough to get any person down.

It was just my luck, though, that my latest delivery had me setting the *Navaplastas* down on Gunnaral-40, and me having to skulk about there on my pudgy legs and all with the package like I was just another *delivery boy*.

Yeah, that got me just a little angry, thinking about it, but nothing compared to how I felt as I headed on back to the terminal, the drop-off complete, only to find a whole trio of kids had latched onto my boot heels and were following me with those wide-eyed stares that I've come to recognise as the look of kids from these planets of misery.

I know that look well because I used to see it in the mirror myself.

These weren't like normal kids, of course, what with their whole depressed demeanour, but they were damn certain persistent in the way that they simply wouldn't stop following me even when I shouted at them near a dozen times.

After all that had failed, I offered them this orange I'd been lugging around in the pocket of my trousers, but they didn't seem interested in that either.

They just watched the orange slip out of my fist and land in the puddle of muck at their feet.

As if they could just let food go to waste.

It was then that I threw up my hands, and resolved just to stick with it, to head on back to the terminal and trust in the guard there to prod the kids with that electric stick of his—stop them from stowing away on the *Nava*.

But then one of the kids, the biggest of the three of them, the one with the mud-splotched cheeks said, "Mr Arkle, can't you help us?"

Well, maybe I shoulda just left things there, just gone on into the terminal, and not stood to attention to *some kid.*

But, sucker that I am, and not without a little ego when it comes to finding how some stranger somehow knows my name, I did stop, looked the kid up and down then said, "What you want?"

The kid seemed to have worked this out quick, that this was something that'd catch my attention, and so he moved sharpish onto the next stage of whatever it was that he had in mind.

He was wearing this kinda shroud sort of thing—not much more than *rags* really—and he shuffled about inside for something he was holding in the pocket there.

It was about that time when I thought about getting a little stricter on my policy of lugging a blaster about planetside . . . I can't tell you the amount of times that I've been caught short without a gun to hand—guess that'll teach me for trusting people.

But the kid didn't pull out no gun, or nothing like that at all.

It was a scrap of paper.

I looked to the faces of the other kids, as if they might be able to give me some sort of a clue about just what was involved here but they weren't giving nothing away.

Just looking kinda flat-expressioned, sort of pale, and unhealthy.

The first kid shoved the note towards my chest.

I kinda felt like I had no option but to take it.

It was a sad little scrap of paper, nothing more than about the size of my palm, and it'd been folded over one time too many and there was now a large tear right through the centre.

The ink of it was blue—and the handwriting scrawly, kinda hard to make out.

But I could read it.

Just.

Captain Wright, I hope you don't mind me having these children bring this message here to you—or that I took liberties in divining your identity—but I would like it very much if you would come to visit me at my home. I have a proposal that might interest you greatly.

Tabby

Well, the name meant nothing to me at all.

Just got me thinking about a cat we once had back home, but no person attached to it that *I* could think of.

All this talk of 'divining' was, quite frankly, alarm-bell stuff for me, oh I've shot through my fair share of planets, sectors of the galaxy, to know what screams: *nutter!*

Then again, this *was* a proposal that might 'interest me greatly' so how could I refuse?

As long as 'interest me greatly' could be substituted with 'pay astronomically' then I guessed it would be just fine.

I told the kids to take me to their leader.

2

ND SO THEY DID.

They led me along a good twenty-minute hike which led right up the hill, which ran alongside the terminal, and up above most of the city, to this odd, ramshackle little house that seemed to have been cobbled together entirely with ersatz wood.

It was painted all white, though it hadn't had a coat for several years, it seemed.

The paint was peeling back to reveal the dirty grain of the wood beneath.

I would've thought that the kids had some interest in mugging me, and I had to remind myself of the note I still held—well, actually, it was scrunched up in my fist—and that this person, whoever this person 'Tabby' was, had worked out my name and who I was.

And my experience with *that* type of person was that they usually had some pretty bulky-ass weapons . . . weapons at least that'd give the *Navaplastas* a good month's worth of nightmares.

I held back at the creaky little metal gate which hung off its hinge, looking a little bit like a hangnail that just invited being tugged right off the rest of the way, and put out of its misery . . . that, I thought, was a pretty adequate term to describe Gunnaral.

The kid who'd handed me the note didn't have such reservations, and he slid on past me to the gate, peeled it back gently, as if he wanted to get all the use out of it that he could, and then he invited me onwards.

Standing up on the elevated front porch, and looking on down at the sad little excuse that Gunnaral called its capital, I breathed in something that smelled a whole lot like raw sewage—and I've had way more experience than I care to remember of *that* smell while way out in the middle of deep space with the *Nava*.

I managed to keep my hamburger lunch down.

But it was a close thing.

The kid thumped his little, malnourished fist up against the front door, and I listened to his pounding echo about inside the front hall of the house.

And then we waited.

And *waited*.

Once I'd got done with my waiting, I glanced on down behind us, back down the hill which consisted pretty much all of broken up asphalt, and to the terminal where I knew the *Nava*: my home, was waiting for me.

If this *was* a ruse then somebody was going to get shot . . . as long as they hadn't hijacked the *Nava* and my blaster to go with it.

We must've stood there on that front porch for a good ten minutes more, and I got to tapping my boot heel against the wooden planks. The wooden planks made a kinda whining, groaning noise, and I sorta got a little fun out of that for a while.

Then, with nothing at all happening, I looked over the kids, said, "Well, thanks very much for this little hike, it was fun while it lasted," and I headed on down the garden path, and off down the hill, already thinking about how the *Nava* must've missed me.

And, what do you know, that was right when the front door thought to open itself.

Well, that wasn't quite it since there was a person there too.

An old woman, actually.

In a kind of blue-grey dressing gown which I guessed, once upon a time, had been soft and white.

She didn't seem to be able to see well at all judging from all the squinting she was doing, how she was doing herself a bit of an effort to get a look at who it was knocking on her door.

"Cookie?" the boy who'd handed me the note said to her.

This seemed to stir her into a mite of action—which, for her, meant a little arthritic shuffle off back into the recesses of her home.

She returned a minute or so later with a cookie for each of the boys, who scuttled off fairly sharpish.

Then the old woman turned to me, smiling of all things, and with them creases showing at the sides of her face and around her eyes, she said, "And you must be Captain Arkle Wright."

"You'd be one-*hundred*-per-cent right on that one ma'am."

3

TEN MINUTES LATER, and sitting in her kitchen with a fresh mug of tea in my hand, and a plateful of cookies near enough demolished, she started into this story of hers.

Turned out that this place, here on Gunnaral-40, of all places, there used to be an FSA base. And that her husband had once served with them. She went on about some other stuff that I either didn't quite follow or didn't quite pay attention to closely enough . . . there was a bunch of cookies for the eating in my defence . . . but the upshot of the whole thing was that her husband had ventured on out on this mission for the FSA and just never come back.

A *real* heart-wrencher, and I'm not even being sarcastic.

I was almost bawling my eyes out.

When she got through with the tale, it was fairly obvious just what she wanted me to do, but I paid attention to her anyway, not wanting to seem rude at having abused her wonderful hospitality.

"Captain Wright, I understand from your signals that *you* once served in the FSA."

I held up my hands, removed them from my still-warm, but now-empty mug of tea then said, "Now, you hang about there just a sec, that's something I wanted to get clear right away . . . how'd you know my name, and who I was?"

She gave a slight smile, and I saw her watery blue eyes gain a bit of a sparkle. "Grahum"—that was her husband's name—"he put in a listening post upstairs, got it put in there by the FSA . . . you see, out here, in his last few years, the FSA pulled their base from Gunnaral, didn't seem to think that it was pulling its weight . . .

but they left Grahum behind here on honorary duty, to keep an ear to the ground, so to speak."

I sat back in my chair, not really sure how I felt about that story.

Though the old woman hadn't given me any reason *not* to trust her, I have to admit that I'm overly cautious with anybody who calls a backwater like Gunnaral-40 home: voluntarily or otherwise.

I decided to believe her, and so I sat forwards, already losing myself in the wonderful thought of being back on the *Nava*, sinking into my springy captain's chair and getting a long way the hell away from Gunnaral-40.

"Captain Wright," she said, "I'd like you to bring him back to me."

Well, I'd be lying if I said that I *hadn't* seen that one coming, but, all the same, when she actually put the offer into words, just what it was that she wanted from me, I couldn't help but give a shrill smile.

"Look," I said, "I know you're no doubt awful lonely here and everything but from what you told me, with him being gone for eight *years* now . . ."

"Eight *months*," she said, correcting me.

"Right," I said, with a greater smile still, "Even with him being gone eight *months*, I can't see that he'll be coming back alive, I mean, if you'll excuse me speaking frankly, ma'am."

She gave a slight nod, and her stare got sort of distant.

Already, I regretted having been so brisk with her.

This was an old *widow* after all, and Arkle Wright is many things but he's not the kinda guy who goes around picking on *widows*.

"I know, Captain," she said, "That's why I was so pleased to see your record—I like it when people speak the truth, tell me just what the *odds* are." She looked back at me, met my eye for a lingering while then added, "And I do realise that the likelihood that he's alive is small." She reached out and snagged a stray thread off her dressing gown. "But I'd just like you to bring him home, that's all."

I sat there stewing on the thing for a long while, trying to work out just what I was going to say. To call this sort of thing a *hopeless* case would've been to put it lightly . . . but I couldn't help feeling a slight tug at my heartstrings.

Call it sentimental, whatever, but I lost good buddies back in the FSA, and so that was why I agreed to the old lady's proposal.

Even waived my fee.

That's how touched I was.

4

JUST LIKE THAT I was flying on out of the terminal of Gunnaral-40—just like I'd wanted all along—but it was with the knowledge that, whatever happened, I'd be heading on back down here before too long.

I checked over my screens, looked up the coordinates that the old lady—that 'Tabby,' as she'd asked me to call her—had posted to the *Nava*.

Almost instantly I could see just how her husband Grahum had got himself all lost.

Where he'd last checked in with his navigational computer was right there on the fringe of the Fritten System, right about that point where things get all screwy from a communications perspective.

The problem with being out there—out right on the edge of the System—is that it's just a prime picking spot for rebels, or gangs, or worse, who'll shoot right over the border, take whatever it is they need, and then jet on back before anybody's had so much as a chance to contact the nearest FSA patrol.

Yeah, these people that live right on the edge of Fritten are parasites of the very worst kind. They ain't got no morals. No real order. They just live on anarchy and on their *animal* instincts. In fact, the only thing that I consider separates them from the animals is them just having spaceships and blasters . . . but that's just *my* take on the thing.

The whole problem, though, for Tabby's husband as I saw it,

and what had most likely hindered any sort of a rescue effort, if the FSA had actually had the resources to go through with one, was that the rebels—the *animals*—they all had their own communication blockers, and made it seem like blackest night beyond the border of the Fritten System.

But it seemed like that *blackest night* was just where I was headed.

Don't you scoff the next time somebody tells you I'm sentimental, because when it comes to helping little old ladies find their disappeared FSA-serving husbands I'm your man.

I rocked on out there, following the pebble trail that Grahum had left for me, and I thought to myself about how it was eight months old, and how there was next to no chance of me being able to divine just where he might've gone.

There was that *divine* word again, and coming right out of my own skull.

I'd have to take care or, before I knew it, I'd end up a blithering, superstitious wreck.

Just like I always do when I blow on over the border of Fritten, I sucked in my gut as if that'd help if some rebel patrol ships decided they'd taken a liking to the *Navaplastas*.

But it was quiet out there.

Just a bunch of empty space.

When I consulted my navigation systems, checking for the personal notes which Grahum had filed after the pebble trail on his ship had quit transmitting, I saw that he'd written down some other coordinates, which I guessed was his proposed course.

I followed them along, keeping an eye out as I went.

To my untrained eye, there was really not much to see.

Not out through the visor, or on my comms systems.

So I decided to slump back in my chair, stick my feet up on the control console and catch a few winks of sleep. From when I'd last calculated it, I hadn't slept for going on twenty hours, and so I deserved just a little.

5

I WOKE with the proximity alarms clanging loudly in my ears.

I scrabbled about, no doubt smacking a bunch of buttons and such that really shouldn't have got smacked.

And when I finally glanced on up to my visor, over to the three-dimensional rendering of the area surrounding the *Nava*, I saw that there was a ship floating about.

In open space.

Quick as I could, I read off the ID.

Found out just as quick that it was an FSA-registered craft.

Another second later, and I got a positive match on it being Grahum's ship.

It was then that I thought to myself that, if the FSA *had* come looking, then they really hadn't looked all that hard.

. . . Or maybe, with Gunnaral being the dump that it was, there simply wasn't a spaceship about ready to be hired till I came along . . . from the way that the officials at the terminal acted with me, the way that they all sorta snapped to attention from their naps, or from tapping away at their entertainment units, it was like they hadn't ever *seen* a spaceship before.

Anyway, I hopped to it, hoping to hell that the walkway on the ship wouldn't be damaged . . . I hadn't tried to fit into my spacesuit for a good long while—for as long as I could help it . . . whenever I ran into any sort of trouble with the *Nava* I had way more sense to duck on into the nearest service station than to go all *floaty-float* outside the ship and try a spot of DIY.

I got everything all lined up—the walkway all lined up—and I sent a request to the ship for the docking.

The *Nava* got back an automatic response, which was just how I expected it.

After all, I had no other expectation *other* than finding a corpse inside of that free-floating ship. Once you've floated about space for a little while you get to the point where a dead human body loses its ability to shock.

But the smell, though, that's a different thing altogether.

You never get used to *that* smell of a body that's been decomposing for a few months.

I waited for the *blip-blip* which informed me that the walkways were aligned and that it was safe to cross. Then, taking a good lungful of the relatively fresh air of the *Nava*, I stepped on out into the walkway, wondering just what I'd find.

6

W HEN I STEPPED ON in through the doorway to the FSA-registered ship, I'd been expecting that smell—the *dead body* smell . . . but that wasn't the case at all.

In fact, from what I could tell, the air had a kind of minty note to it.

And it was *warm* in there too.

So I guessed the systems were still running, at least on backup.

I jabbed my tongue into the side of my cheek, tasting that sort of bloody skinlike taste, still not about to shake the idea that I'd soon come across a dead body lying about here—and *that* odour would hit me, and this place would be Vomit City.

As I walked about, my boots made a sort of echo around me as the sole made contact with the metal grating.

I looked about the entrance hall, trying to work out if there was anything significant.

But, nope, it looked pretty much like any other FSA ship I've had the misfortune to find myself on, which was to say it was pretty much decked out in that *synthetic* white—wall-to-wall—without so much as a poster for variation.

I couldn't help but feel a brief shudder pass over the surface of my skin.

Just thinking about my *own* service in the FSA.

I trod onwards, along the metal grating, still hearing my footsteps echoing about me. As I headed along, I reached down to my thigh holster where I had the grip of my blaster just sticking out there.

Now, I might not be the most *rigorous* when it comes to walking about armed when I go planetside, but that's maybe just because I make it such an obsession to *always* have a blaster handy whenever out in space . . . and *certainly* when stepping onto a strange, apparently drifting ship.

I felt for the rubber grip, allowed my fingers to sort of casually wrap themselves about it, and then I stalked onwards, into the ship.

I found pretty much nothing at all.

It was a standard ship.

A bridge. Eating quarters. That entrance hall I'd passed through.

I guessed that there was maybe—at a stretch—about enough room for four crewmembers to be comfortable for about a month or so of flying time.

When I'd got tired of my snooping, and feeling kinda glad that I wouldn't have to uncover a dead body after all, I headed on back towards the entrance hall.

Way I saw it, the most likely thing was that Grahum had got himself took by some rebels, or something, and they'd maybe shown a little sense not to lug an FSA-registered craft on down to their base.

Because even *animal* rebels understand that an FSA-registered craft has gotta have some tricky tracking system attached.

As I allowed my shoulders to relax just a little, and I turned my thoughts to getting back into the captain's chair of the *Nava*, I heard a sound off over my shoulder.

Nothing more than a *scuttle*.

Like a *rat* or something.

I turned around.

Found myself staring into a quite small—but very *black*—little hole of a blaster.

"You make a move for your blaster, I blow your brains out, son."

7

I HELD STILL—just as still as a larger gentleman, like myself, can manage to hold himself.

And I stared at him.

Read those creased-on wrinkles about his leathered, hide-like skin.

He had wispy, white hair, still full and healthy-looking.

And he wore the uniform of the FSA.

But, for some strange reason, I found my focus kept coming on back to that blaster gun he was pointing right at the tip of my nose.

"That's it," he said—the man who I assumed was Grahum, "Now you toss that blaster down at my feet, ya hear?"

I moved slowly, knowing that I didn't have anywhere *near* the skill to pull off any fancy work with my blaster.

I took hold of the grip between my index finger and thumb, and then, after waiting out a couple of heartbeats, I let it drop.

It landed at the man's feet with a *clang* that echoed all about the otherwise silent ship.

He stooped down to fetch my blaster, and stuffed it into the back of the waistband of his trousers. "Turn around," he said.

I did as he asked, looking off down the walkway, back to my ship, and knowing that if I chose to make a run for it now, he would have no hesitation in shooting me right between the shoulder blades.

He might even have had the skills to get me right in the heart.

Nope, if there's one thing I've learned with people who act all

confident around guns, it's to trust that they are a real sharpshooter
. . . till you get some other idea for sure that they ain't.

I felt him come closer to me, caught a whiff of bad breath, and
then I felt him pad me all over, apparently looking for more
weapons.

Seeming to be satisfied that I wasn't carrying anything else, he
took a few steps back, and then said, "What are you—bounty
hunter?"

"Can I turn round now?"

"Sure."

I turned round, looked to him standing there, that blaster of his
still pointing at my chest. "D'you mind?" I said.

He gave a shrug. "You tell me, son, you're the one that's just
come and set foot on *my* ship."

I decided that was probably the best I was going to get out
of this.

"Fine," I said, "Well, I ain't a bounty hunter—not really—to tell
the truth I came here because your wife asked me to come
fetch you."

I studied his face for any reaction.

Saw none at all.

He kept his gaze fixed on me.

"My wife?" he said, almost snarling out the words, "I ain't *got*
no wife."

Now this whole situation was just getting annoying, and I was
getting a little tired of it, to be honest. I just wanted to get this
through with, bring this man back to his wife, and be done with
the whole deal.

I was even hoping that I might get a pretty nice payoff too.

Just a *polite* tip.

That's right, events had conspired against me to get me thinking about how much I might get paid for this supposed 'nice thing' I was doing here.

"What're you talking about?" I said. "Down there on Gunnaral-40, that's where her house is, that's where she's *waiting* for you—don't you wanna go back and see her, it's been eight months now, pal."

He shook his head, and I noticed how his finger appeared to squeeze the trigger of his blaster just a little.

I felt my stomach crunch in on itself, and those cookies which the woman had given me were maybe, right then, threatening to make a reappearance.

But I held myself still.

Warded off that nauseous feeling.

"Whatcha talking about?" he said, and then, his tone becoming a little more brutal, added, "Who *sent* you?"

I sighed long and hard, knowing space dementia when I saw it, and I said, "Listen, *your wife*, she was the one who sent me here, she was *worried* about you because you've been gone for *eight months*, okay?"

I took a deep breath, never taking my eye off that little hole at the end of the guy's blaster, knowing that I could really *not* do with having my shoulder opened up out here in the middle of the sticks.

"Why dontcha give me a chance?" I said. "A chance to explain —I can tow your ship back to Gunnaral-40 and you can thrash things out with her, how's that sound?"

I felt like I could feel the air between us crackle with static.

In fact, I was almost certain that I felt a spark tickle against my chin.

Why wouldn't this guy just *listen* to me . . . even if he *did* have a dose of crazy going on?

The guy seemed to be considering this.

I watched as his grip on the blaster let off just a touch.

If I'd been of that bent—or maybe a couple of pounds lighter—I might've tried my luck at grabbing for the blaster.

But as things were, and what with that walkway behind me, I didn't want to find myself stranded here in this obviously burned-out ship.

"Tabby?" I said. "You remember her?"

I watched his face for any reaction at all.

He seemed to wince just a touch—just the flinch of a muscle to the side of his left eye.

But he kept on holding the blaster at me, kept it pointing at my chest.

"Never heard that name before," he said.

Finally, I let loose that long-held sigh, and wondered whether I shouldn't just go find myself a nice *desk* job in some *very quiet* colony.

8

WE STOOD LIKE THAT for a long, long while.

And the guy was sort of talking to himself the whole time.

Every few minutes or so, I'd try to bring him round, bring him out of this sickness that obviously had a hold on him, but he just wouldn't shift.

Or so it seemed.

But that was when it struck me—just what I could say to him to bring him out.

"You know," I said, "I served in the FSA too."

The man sneered at me, and I saw him jiggle the blaster just a touch in his tightly held fist. "Nah, you *didn't*."

I shook my head, feeling like I was taking part in some kids' pantomime, or some such. "Yep," I said, "'Fraid so—much younger, though, and *way* lighter. They wanted to give me my own ship and all."

I paused for a second, gauging the guy's reaction—but saw nothing of note.

"I turned them down—thought that I could make ends meet much better alone."

I thought the man might've been on the point of flat-out rejecting my story—or as *I* saw it, my *past*—but instead he said, "And did you?"

"Well," I said, "I get blasters pointed at me from time to time, and I've had my fair share of days when I haven't really known where the next meal was coming from, but, *yeah*, for the most part I've made it." I shrugged. "Got my own ship, and all."

The man looked past me, along the walkway, to the *Nava*. "That your ship?"

"Seems that way, don't it?"

The man didn't seem to mind my sarcasm-inflected tone, and I noticed—for the first time in our standoff—that the blaster was falling down to his side.

Still I knew that I'd never make it back to the *Nava*—not even if I ran . . . nope, the only way I was getting out of that ship was if the guy *let me out*.

"And you . . ." the guy began, staring off at the *Nava* ". . . you *come* all the way out here to fetch me?"

I shrugged. "Seems that way, don't it?"

I watched on as his face creased up in about a thousand different ways, as his brain was—no doubt—doing battle with the truth in the face of delusion.

I had heard all sorts of stories about space dementia, and what might bring it on . . . though I can never confess to having experienced it first-hand myself, from what I've heard it comes about from that feeling of being alone in a great big—*endless*—void, and that if someone was to just cut that fragile rope that ties you onto the rest of mankind, why, you'd just go floating off into it, and be forgotten forever.

Was that what had happened to this guy?

Had he stared into the abyss, and had the abyss bit him back?

Perhaps it was the only explanation that I could work with.

"Come on," I said, "let's get you back to your wife."

9

WITH HIS SHIP IN TOW, we got on back to Gunnaral-40 though I could feel a gut revulsion at having to set foot in the place again.

So, we set on down, his ship parked alongside mine in what musta been just about one of the trickiest landings *I've* ever had to get my head around, and then we climbed on up the hill, headed for his wife's house.

This time there wasn't all that waiting around like before, this time his wife—Tabby—was already out there on a rocker—yep, an *actual* rocker—and looking on out at us with that sort of mid-air stare.

I stopped off at the front gate and allowed the guy to shift past me.

As he went by, I noticed the change in his expression, the way that his eyes seemed to widen up as if he was just seeing something for the first time, like that look I probably get when I forget one of the many—*many*—security protocols for the *Nava* and then, suddenly, just like that, with a kind of *snap*, it comes back to me.

Yep, just like that.

And I just stood by, at the garden gate, and I watched them for a while—the two of them embracing for the longest time.

Well, truth be told, I didn't hang around to see when that hug ended, because I knew that my work was done.

On my way back to the terminal I even caught myself whistling—and I soon put a stop to it. If there's anything worse than tuneless whistling, it's whistling at all, at least in my book.

Nobody really seemed to care all that much as I stepped on up to the *Nava*, sunk myself down in the captain's chair and then fired up the thrusters, ready to take on the next adventure.

And I hoped—for the love of everything that was holy—that it'd pay pretty well.

THE SPECIMEN

1

RULES, RULES, RULES . . . yeah right.

We've all heard the rules, we've all broke them too.

Rules are what keeps us in check, what keeps us getting broke up by some stupid shit, or other. Even when we decide to break the rules it's with good intentions.

Like getting paid.

I'm going to talk about how one of my rules got made: the one that I've got about not carting any living creature on the *Navaplastas*—that's my spaceship. And let me tell you that the rule goes for living creatures escorted or otherwise.

A total no-go.

Just like always with the *real* bad jobs, this one came to me after I'd wheeled out of *The Bitch's Leap* on Hortenine-6 sometime after twentieth hour and I was doing my best to tap my way through the security systems of the *Nava*.

Anybody who's seen the security systems of the *Nava* will know that it's no joke.

I could hardly see straight and I *really* was struggling to hold back the bitter moiser I'd ingested, not to mention keeping the familiar, rich smell of oil from turning my stomach into all sorts of places that a stomach really wasn't meant to go.

I'd just got the third triple *bleep*, the one telling me that if I dared get the password wrong again I'd get a good zapping, when I heard that snivelling, curling voice behind me.

. . . And idiot like I was, I turned around.

Standing on my heels was a lady of about fifty years old. For a long while, I struggled to make the lady stay still, not to mention getting shot of her twin sisters hanging about at the edges. When I did get her somewhat clear, I saw that she had that purple-blue hair that comes from a bad dye job, and she had wrinkles all over her face that made her look a little like a tortoise. I thought that she was about to feed me some line about how I shouldn't drink and pilot, when I noticed the package in her arms.

A wicker basket with an animal inside.

At first, I thought it was one of those lap dogs—those dogs that you can just about cart around in your pocket, if you're that way inclined . . . but I soon caught a glance at a horn, or something, and I guessed that, most likely, it wasn't the case.

There was also the thing that the creature inside of that wicker basket had what looked like lime-green fur sprouting up off its back, and no self-respecting dog I'd ever run into had had fur like that . . . or maybe it was that this dog just didn't have no respect . . . I didn't spend too long staring at the fur, trying to get it straight in my mind, because it was starting to make my head hurt, not to mention making me feel just a little nauseous.

The woman spoke quick, and in a way that, if I'd been any sort of shade of sober, I'd immediately have cottoned onto—got at least *a little* spooked by.

When she did speak, it was out the corner of her mouth as if somebody might be watching on from a distance and she didn't want them to lip read her.

For all I knew somebody *was* watching on.

"Captain?" she said, immediately going right for my sweet spot —even if it is true, any space smuggler worth his salt prefers being addressed as 'Captain' to 'Fleabag,' 'Shitstain' or simply 'Filth' any day of the week, any time, night or day.

"Yes, ma'am," I replied, doing my best to act civil.

"I was wondering if you would be available to deliver my Snookums to Alterbridge-7."

"To Alterbridge-7?" I said, scratching my head. "Ain't that just around the corner from here?" I hadn't even really been much for keeping any sense of direction—I've got navigational systems for a reason, and if I didn't bother to use them I might as well dump them out and save on the weight . . . sure it'd bring my fuel expenses down a little . . .

She smiled back, and I saw she had a little lipstick on her teeth. "Yes, Captain, that's right."

I wanted, more than anything, to scratch my arse, but I knew that in this company that really wouldn't be possible. So, instead, I just scratched my head some more. "Uh, and what're you paying exactly?"

She was paying enough for my moiser-addled mind to get that little voice all excited and, before I knew it, I was carting that creature—wicker basket and all—onto the *Nava* and dumping it into the cargo bay.

If only I knew.

2

THAT SLINKY, RUSTY SOUND of the springs in the captain's chair is one of the sweetest sounds on the *Nava*. It's the sound of home. And with the warm, slick smell of oil and grease all about me, I reached out and took hold of the controls, angling for a straight-up exit out of the terminal. Off of Hortenine-6.

Out of the kitchen, I'd plucked up a porkler—these little jiggly, wormlike things that taste something of meat, and something of mint, and their general purpose is to stop any nosey Fritten System Authorities officer—an FSA officer—from getting up himself and testing out just how sober you really are. Thing is, any self-respecting space smuggler—just like any self-respecting dog—ain't in any way sober. Just the way things are.

So, as I sucked away at the porkler, feeling that meaty, minty tang rumbling its way all over my tongue, I took in the sights of leaving Hortenine-6 . . . and there *are* sights on leaving Hortenine-6 behind . . . or, maybe, to be more accurate, there's *one* sight, and that's the great big billboard that you see as you're blasting on out of the atmosphere, the one which says:

> Thanks for visiting Hortenine-6!
> Have a safe journey!
> Back soon?

For some reason, the 'Back Soon?' part of the sign always raised a smile with me, kind of like it was striking this needy tone of a kid—or maybe an overly attached girlfriend—because, and this is my point, anybody who comes to visit Hortenine-6 for anything *other* than business, there's almost no question that they *won't* be coming back.

And that's to say nothing for the Hortenine-6 dwellers themselves who, poor souls, can't even hardly get clearance to leave their sorry little planet behind.

I know, I'm from a sorry little planet myself . . . Arkle-4 has all the same jokes.

The only reason that Hortenine-6 exists as the centre of the universe for space smugglers is because of *The Bitch's Leap,* where just about all the smuggling business gets done, for good or ill, and make no mistake, where *The Bitch's* is concerned, there's been an awful large amount of 'ill' over the years.

Anyway, I'd just cleared Hortenine-6, always a nice feeling, and I was blasting on out into Big Black—space—paying far more attention to my navigation systems now than the actual controls of the ship. I was headed for Alterbridge-7.

I was paying a whole lot more attention to my navigational systems because it'd shown up, four straight times in a row now, that there wasn't such a place as Alterbridge-7.

I furrowed my brow and did what I always do when the navigational systems of the *Nava* seem to be having a little laugh at my expense.

I gave it a smack.

The screen did that quivering thing where waves of static passed across the display, but I knew that it was only for show, that the display wasn't *really* shook up. Well, that was really to say that, if I'd really wanted to, I could shake it up a whole lot more.

I could really rock the navigational systems' world if I liked.

And that'd leave me pretty much stranded too.

Just about the only place that I know how to get my way to without the navigational systems is *The Bitch's Leap*.

I tapped Alterbridge-7 into the interface again, and got the same message back.

No dice.

No matter what I did.

I drew in a deep breath and then sighed it right back out again.

As per the terms of the deal I'd struck with the old lady, she'd paid me half up front and then there would be somebody accepting the shipment to pay the other half. That's another thing about taking jobs while drunk, it gets you doing some really stupid shit. I think even a week before that particular incident, I'd decided myself that I wouldn't take on any more jobs drunk. Thing is that you've gotta make sure you get paid everything right up front. None of this *split* payment crap for me, thank you very much.

Well, you live and learn, I guess.

And I *was* doing a lot of learning right there and then, fiddling about with my navigational systems.

When I'd got through with all the swearing—not to mention a whole lot more of pounding on the navigational systems—I had something of a clear head apart from all the moiser still rushing about my veins and keeping me stinking drunk.

I stood there, on the bridge, something catching my attention.

The thing about a moiser stupor is that, often, and for a long while, you're pretty much numbed to the outside world, and when the outside world tries to get through to you it's about as effective as a whisper from across a thousand-mile forest.

But, this time, I could certainly hear something.

In fact, I could hear enough of it to know that it was a *clunking* sound.

I shifted around, looked to the doorway of the bridge.

There was nothing there, of course, acting as a sole traveller I was the only one on the ship . . . besides the dog-creature thing in the wicker basket.

I wonder if I'd maybe throttled the *Nava* a bit too hard coming out of Hortenine-6 and I'd managed to snap something important in the process.

That could be it.

It'd happened before.

But this clunking was different in some way.

With all my experience of dealing with broken bits of space ships—and that's a pretty long and hard-won experience, let me tell you—I'd never quite heard anything being so *loud* and, well, so *percussive*. It sounded like there was something big, and back *there*, in the cargo bay, making a great big racket.

Whatever it was, it sounded pissed off.

I scrabbled about down under my controls and uncovered my burned-up space blaster. It wasn't all that much, not much more than a standard piece of gear bought off a black market here or there, but it had been modified in such a way that it would pack a real punch if it had to . . . just as long as there wasn't any sharp-shooting to be done, I'd be fine.

Blaster in hand, I squeezed my way out off the bridge and down along the corridor in the direction of the kerfuffle.

The clunking got louder and louder as I made my way down the corridor. I gripped my blaster tighter still, telling myself that I just had to shoot the damn thing—because surely it was the dog, or whatever—that had got loose and be done.

I could feel my palms getting all sticky with sweat, and my heart hammering at my throat. At some point along the way, I'd swallowed my porkler, so now I only had that dry, bloody taste remaining in my mouth . . . with the faintest suggestion of mint.

Just like in the whole of the *Nava,* the way to the cargo hold smelled thickly of oil and grease, and I could feel it making my nostril hairs tingle.

But I tried not to think about that.

I tried to *think* sober.

When I get drunk I have this *thing* I do—the way I like to think of it is that it's something along the lines of imagining just about every single scenario that could possibly play out. Yeah, I was doing that right then. And it was, to be quite frank, getting to be a little annoying. Because I knew that all I really needed was to squeeze the trigger in the general direction of the nuisance.

I stood at the entrance to the cargo bay, blaster raised now, and ready to jam my fist into the switch right there on the wall. I drew a breath. Another. And another.

Then, with the biggest *clunk!* of them all, one which made the whole ship tremble, I tumbled right down to the ground.

3

I MUST'VE BLACKED OUT for a clean few seconds, because when I came to, the whole of the *Nava* was shaking and I realised that the cargo door was no longer shut . . . actually, taking another moment to inspect my surroundings a little better, I realised that the cargo door wasn't *there* anymore.

I padded around for my blaster.

Found it lying nearby.

I grabbed hold of it.

Spun around.

Tried to locate the source of this thing.

No luck.

I glanced back into the cargo bay, off into the gloom there.

Nothing I could see.

I drew in another breath, spun around.

And right there, before my eyes, I saw the creature.

Oh, it had the green fur that I'd spotted from before, and I could see that it in some way resembled the little doggy thing that'd been inside of the wicker basket, but I could also see that it was now a clear few feet taller than I was. And that, maybe the most alarming thing of all, it was walking up on its hind paws.

I stared at the thing.

The thing stared at me.

We stared at one another.

I raised my blaster up and fired.

The kickback sent me into the wall behind.

I felt the impact at the centre of my spine.

All the air left my lungs as I tumbled down to the floor and landed with a *bump*.

I found myself looking up at the creature above me.

I saw that I'd made no mark at all with my blaster pistol, and I couldn't help feeling just a touch gutted about the whole thing . . . I mean, when you fix to shoot something good and proper, you sort of expect it to do the decent thing and die.

This creature, though, it seemed, had no intention of dying at all.

While I was awaiting my death, I got a bit of a better look at the creature.

Green fur.

Yeah, I'd got that all checked off already.

And then there was the face, a little like a dog's, with that snout and everything, and the wet muzzle, or whatever it was. Then there were the teeth, yep, sharp, pointed, and all that. Finally there were the claws which hung off its paws sort of like thick, very sharp knives.

I had to admit that I wasn't feeling all that confident in my ability to get the job done at that point . . .

I looked about for my blaster, wondering if it might be worth another shot just to check if I'd maybe not caught the creature properly the first time.

But my blaster was way over on the other side of the corridor.

There wasn't much chance of me being able to sweep it up now.

That ship, as they say, had well and truly *sailed*.

I sort of focussed in on one of those claws, and wondered just how it might feel to have the thing penetrating my chest, or gut, or head, whichever this creature decided to go for.

But then it spoke—oh, *man*, did it speak!

"Huuuuman," the creature said.

When it spoke, it had a sort of dog's voice, almost like it was howling out the words.

If there's anything worse than finding yourself alone in the middle of space with a creature a clear head and shoulders taller than you, it's when you find out that said creature can not only communicate with you . . . but that it can speak in *your* language.

"Uh," I said, eyeing any hope of escape, and quickly discarding anything that my moiser-soaked brain could come up with in this pinch, "Yeah?"

The creature glowered at me with its doglike, black eyes.

I really would've liked, more than anything at that point, to have been afforded the opportunity of looking away. But I also knew that if I *dared* to look away then it quite likely would be the very last thing I would do.

Like, ever.

So I forced myself to stare back into those beady black eyes.

"Yoooou," the creature continued, elongating its *o's* in that howling way it had, "Are tooo take me tooo the destination."

I felt myself prickling all over, and I wondered if, maybe, this was some sort of a moiser-induced hallucination. I had had those before . . . but it usually involved either my mother scolding me, or some scorned lover back from the dead.

Still, the creature seemed insistent, so I decided on speaking the truth. "Uh, can't find it on my navigational systems, buddy, sorry to say. If you want to tell me where you need dropping off I'd be only too happy to do so."

And I guess that I've never before spoken words so from my heart.

Words that I *really*—deep down—meant.

The creature seemed to consider this, and then spoke again.

"Take me tooo the bridge."

Now I only stayed slumped up against the wall for so long because I was having a hard time processing the scene that was playing out here, in the poor, old *Nava*. But the creature, it seemed, took that hesitation of mine as a sort of sign of some kind of rebellion.

It shanked over me, crouched down and, with the tip of its claw, scratched me beneath the chin.

Right away, I could feel the blood oozing out: thick and warm and *icky*.

Over the top of the oil and grease of the ship, I could smell the musky fur of the creature standing above me, and then, over that, the scent of my own blood.

I felt like my whole body was cooling.

"Yoooou want payment, dooo you not?"

I have to admit that I was a little more preoccupied with the blood that was still oozing right out of my chin so I didn't answer right away. And when I did finally get my thoughts together enough so that I *could* answer, I managed only a nod.

"Goood," the creature said. "Then take me there."

So I did.

4

NOW, I've been through some surreal things in my time, but certainly having that green, furry monster up there on the bridge with me would surely take some beating.

But who was I to kick up a fuss?

It wasn't like the creature didn't know what it was doing.

It had me sit at the controls and guide the ship along according to its specific instructions. And I did my best to fly him there.

It turned out that Alterbridge-7 wasn't listed on the directory of my navigational systems. And, I have to admit, that shook up my confidence in those systems just a touch. I mean, what's the point of having navigational systems at all if they won't navigate?

The only little hiccup came when the creature pointed out ahead of us—out at what looked to me to simply be empty space— and said, "There."

I think that I was beginning to catch a clue about just *why* Alterbridge-7 hadn't been listed on the navigational systems.

But I allowed the creature to do the explaining.

If there's one thing I've learned about speaking, it's better to wait till you know the full picture before slitting open those lips and sprouting idiocies.

Because it was clear—right here and now—that the creature was very much the one in the driving seat.

"May I?" the creature said, indicating the captain's chair and, by extension, the controls.

Now, I'm a captain just like all the rest, and if there's one thing that rankles a captain more than being asked to 'step aside' and let somebody else drive, then I don't want to hear of it. But the fact that the creature had asked so politely, and maybe also the fact that I knew it could quite easily slit my throat at a moment of its choosing, made me only happy to stand up and allow the creature to take up its place in the captain's chair.

I just stood back and watched on.

The creature angled the controls about, using the throttle with expert precision . . . or maybe it was just normal precision since I hadn't really ever seen much precision about the *Nava*. It kept on steering us into empty space, though I didn't have the heart to tell it . . . or perhaps it was the fact that I still *had* a heart, and really didn't want to encourage it to stab it out of me.

We slowed some more on our way, apparently reaching some unseen point—at least for me—that signalled our destination was approaching.

I only watched on.

The creature was bringing us into a sort of landing pattern, that much I could tell, and I'm not ashamed to admit that I was just a touch jealous to think that even with its claws, its big muscular arms that were clearly unsuited to the controls of my particular ship, that the creature had a delicacy that I simply couldn't emulate.

We were still in open space.

But stopped now.

The creature glanced back over its shoulder at me—it might've been smiling, but I can't say that I could really tell for sure. "Thank yooou, captain," it said, and got up from the controls.

As it headed off the bridge—and maybe it was the moiser, or perhaps it was just all the nerves all bundled up inside—but I couldn't help but call out to it, "Uh, you're just going to step out into space?"

The creature paused in the doorway, long enough for me to realise that it'd been a mistake to say anything at all since it was clear that the creature was leaving . . . and without having killed me.

The creature seemed to be smiling again, though, and it said, "Yooou cannot see in multiple dimensions, can yooou?"

I shook my head.

The creature seemed to take this as a sort of farewell, and it trudged itself out of the ship and—as far as I could tell—right out into open space.

The payment issue only came to me when I'd be flying for a good long time away from the drop-off point. I couldn't believe that I was still thinking about credits when I'd barely escaped with my life from that creature . . . but—hey—I guess a space smuggler is born to do what he does best.

Just curious, not much else, I headed off into the cargo bay, uncovered the wicker basket there. I prised open the lid and I peered inside of it. Sure as shit, there was my payment—the other half the old lady had promised to me—looking just about as beautiful as money can look . . . and I've seen some *pretty* money in my time, let me tell you.

Needless to say, I shot the wicker basket out into space—after I'd relieved it of its credits, of course—I didn't want to be reminded of that whole sorry episode every time I caught sight of it in the cargo bay among the rest of the crap there.

But there's a lesson there, for all of us space smugglers.

Don't ship animals.

TRUTHSAYERS
CONVENTION

1

PERHAPS the *most* defining characteristic of the space smuggler is how they'll do anything for cash. Now, I didn't say *just about* anything . . . I said *anything* at all.

Which brings me to the latest escapade:

Truthsayers Convention.

Now, don't get me wrong, I haven't suddenly up and gone all crazy. Got myself all ensnared with some sort of a cult; truly the worst kind. No, nothing like that. But the truth is sometimes a fearsome beast and one which, when looked in the eye, drives you into making decisions which're based on practicalities and nothing more.

My particular truth turned out to be how I'd been hanging around the Interstellar Hires Bay on Klun-9—as any self-respecting smuggler might do—when I noticed this fella in a sharp suit passing me by a dozen or so times, eyeing me up each time. When he finally stopped to chat with me, I have to admit that I heard a whole heap of nothing except for the price he quoted in credits.

That I heard *all* too well.

In fact, if I recall correctly, I escorted him all the way to my ship—the *Navaplastas*—looking about with jealous anxiety, sure that some other smuggler might descend upon my client and snatch him out of my grasp. But I got him to the *Nava* just fine . . . and he fed me the directions; along with the first half of that hefty payment of his.

I suppose that things all went swimmingly until I got the *Nava* set down planetside—on one of those planets which'd been renamed; its ownership reassigned; according to the whims of some corporation. The planet was simply named Truthsayers Convention.

Now, as a smuggler, I learn an awful deal about human nature.

More specifically the *scams* which crop up time and again.

It shouldn't be said that it's the scammers themselves who're lacking in originality—any sort of creativity. On the contrary, I guess that, in a way, they should be applauded. If the original scams work so well, and over and over again—fooling people effortlessly—then why should they go to all the mental expense of thinking of something new? From my experience, scammers don't tend to be show-offs. They're more in the line of wanting to make a dishonest fortune, here or there . . . that in mind, I don't suppose they're all that different from smugglers . . .

Anyway, I set the *Nava* down in the terminal of Truthsayers Convention, which turned out to be this planet bristling with rain-forests across the entirety of its surface. The terminal itself was all made of wood and set up in a canopy. One of the more *organic* places I've set the *Nava* down on through the course of the years.

As I clambered on out of my ship, I couldn't help but notice the rooftops of other large structures poking up through the canopy; all of them resembling kind of skyscrapers but made of wood.

I'd seen nothing like it in my entire life.

With my client treading along at my side, jabbering on about this and that, I started to have some reservations. I think it was the point when my client reached into the breast pocket of his jacket and handed me over this clip-on nametag with the message: *Hi!*

I'm Arkle! twinkling back at me with the finest in micro light-bulb technology. Yep, it must've been right about that point when I turned to my client, and said, "Uh, what in *good* hell is this?"

My client—his hair blond, and with a well-clipped goatee of the same colour—just flashed his computer-designed smile, and assured me, in some honey-smooth tones, that it was 'for the convention'.

"What convention?" I asked.

My client shrugged his shoulders, smiled, then carried on; going at a faster pace than before.

I know that was the point when I should've cut and run, but I'm nothing if not a sucker for credits. If there's one thing I prize above credits, it's *more* credits . . . and this guy certainly had many a handful. Perhaps one day I'll manage to get myself shot of my credit addiction.

To get into the building beyond the terminal, we had to pass through a couple of security 'bots; nothing major . . . at least nothing which I wouldn't have expected to pass through on the way into some planet's administrative centre; which was what I guessed this place to be.

How wrong I was.

Once I'd cleared security, and had my client still pacing on ahead, I noticed the large desk which occupied much of the wall in front of us. And I saw that there was a red-haired secretary sitting there; blinking all over the place as she spoke to this or that person through a retina display only she could see . . . again, another thing I've learned with experience is that people who voluntarily fit their brains with hardware are *well worth* avoiding.

It was at this point that my client made eye contact with the secretary, who, in turn, nodded back to him. I can't say precisely what I was expecting—perhaps a net to drop down on me from above, capturing me—but it wasn't anything positive. Nothing which was going to improve my life.

So it was with an aching heart that I watched the secretary remove something from my client's upturned palm before he slipped away; a sly grin on his lips while I caught him doing a silent fist-pump as the door wheeled open for him. All I could do was stare after my client and silently berate myself for having accepted his advice to leave my blaster in the *Nava* . . . again, those *damn* credits are my greatest weakness.

"Mr Wright?"

I turned to look at the secretary. "*Captain* Wright."

The secretary beamed back at me in a numbskull sort of way. "The floor is through this way," she said, pointing off towards a door in the other direction to where my client had headed.

I held up my hands. "Whoa, whoa, whoa! I'm not going anywhere, missy, not till I get some sort of an explanation. Certain promises were made. Deals struck. Etcetera, etcetera."

"Mr Wright."

"*Captain* Wright," I again corrected.

"On your acceptance of the 'joining gift' you are now contracted to us for the next month."

"The next *month!*" I just about spat out.

The secretary didn't so much as bat an eyelash. Apparently she wasn't getting any work done on her retina display while she held this conversation with me. I guess I should've been thankful for that minor courtesy. "If you'd read the terms and conditions before . . ."

I wheeled around, headed back out the way I'd come in.

At least I'd got myself the upfront payment.

As I closed in on the doorway, however, I found myself facing off with one of the aforementioned security 'bots. It blocked my path with that two-legged gait; its two barrels of its rifle blasters pointing me right between the eyes.

I backed my way towards the secretary again.

Looked her over.

Gave a slight smirk.

"Uh, all right," I got out.

I glanced over to the door where my client had headed. Then I looked to the secretary's fingers. She was pointing to the door in the opposite direction.

I looked to those twin barrels of the security 'bot's rifles one final time.

Then relented.

2

I SUPPOSE I had half a thought that I'd find myself on some kind of a conveyor belt, facing off with some sort of grisly, industrial food processor. I'd be lying if I said this would be the first time some far-flung nutcases had tried to turn me into hamburgers.

Maybe I should've been pleasantly surprised that that wasn't the case; that, actually, what faced me off on the other side wasn't anything but the main floor of a conference centre. I mean, there was a whole bunch of those booths all set up; everything awash with colour and with people jabbering on at the tops of their lungs. The room was pretty packed and I could feel the body heat rippling through the air. Among all those faces, I could make out nothing save for smiling mouths; rapidly clicking teeth. I couldn't quite shake the feeling that everybody in the room was on *ten* . . . all of them pouring everything they had into the people before them.

Before I'd properly got my mind wrapped around this beleaguering scene, I felt someone tap me on the shoulder. Idiot me, I half expected to find my client standing there, telling me to come with him, and that this had just been some kind of ill-judged joke.

But, nope, it wasn't my client.

It was a young, brunette woman with a smile to match all those on the floor of the convention centre. "Mr Wright?" she said.

"*Captain* Wright," I replied, although this time my voice wasn't as forceful as it had been before, when I'd gone to the trouble of correcting the secretary. I was still somewhat taken aback by the scene which confronted me.

"Let's get you *initiated*, shall we?"

" 'Initiated' ?" I just about got out as she grabbed me by the crook of my elbow and dragged me on away from the rest of the people.

The woman's firm hold on me took me off guard, and I almost tripped over a half dozen or so times as she led the way. I thought about asking her to let me loose but decided, given the thronging masses on either side, that I was better off not getting lost.

The woman finally—*inevitably?*—brought me before my own little booth.

I stared at it.

And, for all I knew, *it* stared back at me.

. . . Never can be too certain just what's inanimate and what's not in *this* universe.

"Here you are, Mr Wright," she said, still smiling, and slipping me only the most sidelong of glances. "In that box there"—she gestured towards a cardboard box—"you'll find everything you'll need to put on a good—*professional*—display. At the end of the day, your ratings will be collated with the rest of the floor and your ranking determined." She turned back to me, meeting my eye directly for what might've been the first time. "Any questions?"

"Uh, yeah, a few . . ." I managed, but it was then that I felt a sharp pain in my hand. "Ow!"

But she was already walking away.

I glanced down at my palm briefly, seeing that there was a sort of staple sticking out of my skin.

As she trotted out of sight, the device she'd used to staple me with down at her thigh, I heard her voice cutting through the champering babble of the conference centre. "You'll find us very helpful—willing to give newbies a hand whenever they need one. You've only to ask . . ."

I watched on as she disappeared among a crowd and knew that I was truly alone.

I turned my attention to my cardboard box, breathed out a heavy sigh, and then yanked back the flaps.

3

I'M NOT ENTIRELY SURE what I expected to find within the box. Maybe I had some secret fantasy that—*somehow*—the conference administration might've overlooked something and, by accident, left a blaster within. Although I've hardly ever been the handiest in the universe with a blaster, I fancied my chances of busting out of the place on the back of sheer exhilaration . . . or, at least, spitting off some sparks for as long as those security 'bots would allow me.

What was actually inside the box was a uniform: a standard set of lime-green overalls which did nothing for my *sizeable* figure. Not seeing anything else open to me at that time, I set about designing my booth as best I could.

I've always been somewhat partial to purple.

Not really sure why.

So when I saw the option to throw up some purple streamers, I took my chances. Then it was only a baby step from there for me to pick a mauve spread for the booth table. I found a whole stack of Dynamic Paper™ within the box too, and guessed that I was meant to program the stuff with promotional material . . . whatever it was we were selling . . .

Before I had a chance to really get a second look—let alone a second *opinion*—on my booth design, I noticed a trio of people had cropped up outside; looking on at my booth in a way that a horde of hungry children might peer in hopefully through the steamed-up windows of a bakery. I turned to them, then reminded myself to smile. "Uh, hi," I got out.

One of the people snorted and then left.

I hoped, for their sake, they were going to the toilets to get themselves a tissue for that nasty-sounding cold of theirs.

Two people remained—a man and woman; and, from the looks of how they half embraced one another: a *married* couple.

I blinked at them.

And they blinked back at me.

I dialled my smile up a little, then said, "Uh, have you seen the material?"

The woman glanced to the man, the husband, and then stepped forwards. She took up one of the pieces of Dynamic Paper^{TM}, leafed through it absentmindedly, and then glanced to her husband.

He looked back at her, stepped forwards, and took one up for himself.

The two of them silently tapped through their promotional material, drinking in the contents as if it was some kind of addictive substance.

Finally, the woman glanced up. She put her hand in the air as if this was some sort of a classroom. "A question?"

I gave a slight smirk before I even knew I was doing it. "Uh-huh."

"When we complete the Process, will we be *assured* success?"

I went with, "Uh . . ." and then glanced to her husband, seeing that he was staring at me just as intently. Finally, I dished out a, "Yeah"—scratched the back of my neck—"*sure.*"

I even threw in a fresh, false smile for the two of them.

The woman seemed unsure for a couple of moments, apparently caught with something else in mind. Finally, though, she looked to her husband, smiled, then gave a nod. She turned back to me. "We'll take two."

" 'Two' ?" I replied, then realised that, as a salesman, I really shouldn't sound *that* surprised.

I managed to snap out of it, and dug out a device I'd been given as part of my cardboard-box setup. I tapped the screen which said: *TAP HERE TO MAKE PURCHASE* and a couple of bright red plastic tokens printed off. Since I wasn't ready for them, they both tumbled onto the floor, landing with plasticky clicks. I moved quickly to stoop over and retrieve them, handing one each over to the man and the lady. "Pleasure doing business with you," I said, again doing my best to smile as I handed over the plastic chips.

The husband and wife wandered away together, chatting.

As I stood there, watching them go, I couldn't help but notice the person from the booth opposite me near enough staring holes in my skull. It was a man. About seventy; maybe eighty. He was wearing a neat suit with a black tie. More than anything else, he looked like a funeral director. His thin—*near-inexistent*—grey hair was slicked to one side of his scalp. As if I'd gone and invited him over, he trod towards me, eyes nearly tumbling free from their sockets. "You," he said, his voice raspy, harsh.

"Me," I agreed.

"*You* . . . two sales—your first *day* . . . and you don't have the first *clue* about what you are doing."

Not having anything to say in my defence, I remained silent. I've always maintained, even before that experience, that smugglers were somewhat higher up on the totem pole when compared to salesmen . . . at least a smuggler's honest about what he does . . . *most* of the time . . .

"You're right, no clue at all. Nobody thought to clue me in."

The man shook his head. "And just why would anyone think to *clue you in?*"

I shrugged. "Politeness?"

The man huffed up his cheeks then he glanced about the conference centre, to all the other people barking at the clients gathered about their booths. I could see that some of the booths had tonnes of people around them, all of them apparently enraptured by whatever it was that the sellers had to say. "It took me a whole *month* before I made my first sale. And then another year before I made the next one." He pointed a finger up at his face. "I was *young* when I first arrived here."

I wasn't certain what to make of this information, as terrifying as it sounded.

So I just scratched my arse a little.

The man turned back to me. "You do realise what you're in for, don't you?"

"No."

The man sighed. "Truthsayers Convention is one of the *most notorious* work schemes in the entire universe."

"Is it now?" I said, my ears perking up a touch . . . I supposed this guy hadn't been entirely wasting his time here, and that he'd put some effort into beefing up his sales language—learning how to make others pay attention to what he had to say.

"How it works," the man said, "is that people arrive here, to the planet, wanting to get some *truth* said about themselves—something which will hopefully illuminate how they might turn their lives around. *Raw honesty.*"

I stared back at the man. "All I can see getting done here, on this shop floor, is a whole bunch of pamphleteering."

The man grinned at me slyly. "Yes, of course, that's because the services are upstairs." Here he jabbed his finger upwards to—apparently—indicate the next floor up. "If you get your work done down here, if you can get *ranked* in the top percentile, then you can graduate."

"And after that? After I get upstairs?"

The man coloured. He averted his gaze. In a voice almost too quiet for me to hear, he muttered, "Don't know—never *made* it there, did I?"

I stared out across the room, and then, from some distant spot out of sight, I heard the *clang-clang-clang* of an out-of-tune bell.

The man turned back to his booth. "Well, that's it for another day."

I watched on as a screen appeared out of thin air.

A whole host of names wrote themselves on the screen.

It took me a while, but I found my own; listed somewhere near the bottom . . . but not *quite* at the bottom . . .

I turned back to the man. "Say, how about we team up on this thing, huh?"

4

A T FIRST the old man was reluctant about striking a deal. He clearly had his pride, having been down on this conference centre floor for the best part of his life. But, in the end, he saw sense in a sort of defeated way and accepted my help.

He turned out to be called Sally—a name which he told me *not* to ask about—and he was actually sort of friendly in a standoffish sort of way. I suppose that having seen so many others 'graduate' the shop floor, going ahead of him, had ground his optimism down over the years. He clearly believed that his time had come, and gone, a long while ago.

As we got to talking, I found out that, unlike me, Sally had actually turned up to this planet out of curiosity. He had been offered a job by Truthsayers Convention and he had accepted. When I told him about the client I'd picked up and about that little scene where they'd had the staple removed from their palm, he met my gaze. "That must be the deal," he said.

"What *deal?*"

"The staple," he said, nodding to my hand; still sore from where that woman had punctured my skin. "They'll take it out if they bring back someone else . . . someone to replace them."

I held my palm up and peered at my skin, at the staple there. "And just what the hell does this thing actually do?"

"It's used to monitor us, and it carries a lethal electrical charge if improperly removed, or tampered with."

"Yeah, right," I said, another smirk lining my lips.

Sally shrugged his shoulders, flashed his eyebrows. "Why not give it a go?"

I stared at the staple imbedded in my palm, thought long and hard about calling Sally's bluff, and then decided against it. If there's one thing I've learned in all my years of smuggling it's that if you find yourself in a position such as this one, where it's clear that certain secrets are being withheld, that a home advantage is being played up to, then you're *far* better off playing by the rules of the home team.

The way we decided to manage our joint efforts at getting to the next floor of Truthsayers Convention was with me on décor. It turned out that Sally had greatly admired the purple shades with which I'd adorned my booth. It was decided I'd pull off the same trick with Sally's booth, then, when it came down to the selling portion, Sally would take over; sending half of them my way so that we'd each receive credit for the customers we attracted.

Now, I'm not a dummy, no matter how it might look, and I knew that, between the two of us, we'd most probably need to attract double the customers of any other Truthsayers Representative to have a chance of finishing in the top percentile. But, from what I'd seen already, the whole conference centre seemed a total snake pit of individuals. The whole Truthsayers Convention seemed to depend on the representatives playing off against one another.

They didn't account for teamwork . . .

When the next day began, that same bell striking its flat note, I went into overdrive, throwing together every last scrap of thought I could muster into making our booths stand out. And it seemed to work, bringing a whole host of people over to mine and Sally's booths.

I guessed that all the mental effort I'd invested over the years into making my ship look better was starting to pay off.

When it became obvious that I was getting out of my depth with questions from the customers, Sally would step in and help me along.

We split the credit fifty-fifty.

I was still jabbering on about this or that, while busy printing off a stack of ten tokens to hand over to customers for the next floor, when I heard the bell clang again. I didn't even turn my head in the direction of the screen which appeared in thin air because I was so swept up in printing off another few tokens. But, when I did, the surprise was an extremely pleasant one.

Me and Sally were sitting on top of the leader board.

Both of us with more than *double* what the next competitors had achieved that day.

On impulse, I slapped Sally a high-five, even though it looked like too many more of those would kill him. The two of us were grinning from ear to ear as the loudspeaker announced those who'd come top of the leader board that day. However, instead of reeling off our names among those who would be promoted to the next floor up, there was nothing but a deafening silence to follow.

It was only when I heard the whining grind of gears and pistons, and hydraulics, that I turned to see a pair of security 'bots appear from out among the crowd. Their rifles were pointed at me and Sally but I knew more sense than to try and run.

Those things could most likely shoot the nose off a cat two systems away.

So like a good little coward I raised my hands in surrender.

Beside me, I saw that Sally had the same good sense.

The security 'bots shepherded us through the dwindling crowds; several of those who had been our customers throughout the day were gawping at us, clearly confused at what was going on.

I held my same *salesman's* smile. I even managed a couple of, "How're you doing, folks?" to nobody in particular.

Finally, the 'bots led us to a room off the conference centre.

Within, a fat, bald man in an ill-fitting suit, two sizes too big, stared at us over his desk. He held his hands clasped tightly together. I heard the door swish shut behind us and the security 'bots, apparently, waiting outside. Although there were no windows in the room, I could see that the walls were the latest in Dynamic Paper^{TM} and that they could be animated with whatever matched the user's whim. Now, though, they were set to a neutral, standby, grey.

Awaiting user input.

I guessed that, once this meeting had run its course, Fatty would program whatever he felt fit . . . whatever might match his mood.

"You two," Fatty said, "have gone about your task in *quite* an unorthodox manner."

Not knowing what to say, and knowing that nothing was more annoying for a middle-manager than talkback, I held my lips sealed.

Fatty leaned forwards in his chair, making its articulations creak, and, at the same time, bringing forth a puff of air from his chest. He eyed the two of us with his tiny, black, piggy eyes.

"Thing is," he said, "I can only let one of the two of you go through."

I felt my chest tighten.

When I slipped Sally a glance, I expected him to be feeding me a hopeful look, one which said something along the lines of this being *his* time—and that I should gracefully step aside. But all I saw in his expression was a complete absence of emotion.

He just wanted this over and done with.

However that might be.

Fatty eyed me closely, with a certain dislike, then turned to Sally. "You can go."

I readied myself to protest, although I still wasn't quite sure what I was protesting *about*.

Sally, though, butted in. "Please, if anybody should go up to the next floor then it should be Arkle . . . without him I never would've thought for us to work together . . . I never would've come up with the *scheme*."

Fatty reached up and massaged his wrinkled temples. He seemed like a man who had way too much to think about to be dealing with us on top of it. "How long you been working here?"

Sally blinked rapidly. Then he glanced to me, as if *I* had the answer to the question. Finally he replied, "Fifty-nine years."

To my ears, hearing that number made my gut sink.

When I looked to Fatty, though, he only pouted nonchalantly. "We let people off with a pension after twenty—you shoulda said something."

I glanced to Sally. He didn't show much of any expression. He simply remained dead-eyed.

The place where emotion went to die.

"You mean I can go?"

"Uh-huh," Fatty said, turning to some screen on his desk, and, with a few deft flicks of his fingers, ordering something or other done.

Sally remained standing at my side for a long while, and then he reached out. Clasped hold of my hand. *Shook it.* He beamed. "Thank you, Arkle. Thank you *so* much!"

And, with that, before I had a chance to remind him that if he'd only said something forty-odd years ago he'd would've gone free, he blasted clear of the office—out through the doors.

Leaving me alone.

Without looking up from his work, Fatty said, "You'll start first thing tomorrow on the programme; on the actual Truthsaying. Best get some rest."

I stood there, still before his desk.

Finally, Fatty glanced up. "What?"

"It's just I don't know anything *about* Truthsaying."

Fatty shrugged. "You'll pick it up." He returned his gaze downwards. "Or else we'll let you go on a pension after twenty years like him."

5

THE NEXT DAY, after a fitful night's sleep in one of the dormitories—different, slightly more expansive than the ones I'd slept in while down on the conference centre floor—I got myself up and over to what would be the day's job.

The next floor up was significantly smaller than the one downstairs, with only about fifteen or twenty booths. Each of these booths was staffed by someone who had, apparently, graduated from the floor below like I had.

None of the customers had yet arrived here and I had a chance to get myself acquainted with my surroundings. What surprised me the most about this floor was how everybody sat in total silence. Every last one of them staring out in front, at the air before their noses. I decided to break the silence. "Uh, you think one of you . . ."

A violent "*Shh!*" brought me to an abrupt halt.

I waited out a few heartbeats and then tried again. "It's just that . . ."

"*Shh!*"

This time I held myself silent.

Then tried again, this time in an obnoxiously loud voice. "Look here, I ain't got the first *clue* about what's going on—or what I'm meant to do to *Truthsay* people . . ." I waited to be silenced again, but this time there was no interruption ". . . do you not think *one* of you could at least give me some pointers?"

A long, long pause in the room. I thought that I actually did hear a pin drop. And then, in a whispering voice I heard the comment; almost so quiet that it drifted down beneath the level of my hearing. "Tell them what they want to hear."

"Huh?" I replied, more out of surprise at the broken silence than anything else.

But there was no follow-up.

I'd heard what I'd heard.

Outside the door, I heard the scrub of shoes on carpet. And then I watched on as the first of the customers wandered on in through. They were skittish types: men and women dressed in try-too-hard overalls with try-too-hard hair and try-too-hard smiles.

I thought back on the wisdom of the advice I'd been given.

And *my* particular wisdom in taking it.

I mean, surely the only reason I'd ever managed to get off the bottom floor was because I'd done exactly what everyone else *wasn't* doing. Why wouldn't pulling the same trick work again?

As I sat there, in my booth, I listened to the first forays of the other Truthsayers.

" . . . You have a solid, square jaw . . ."

". . . Your figure is most womanly—very *shapely* . . ."

". . . If I was hiring, I'd pick someone with your nose right away . . ."

Before I'd even had a chance to properly register just what the hell was going on, I found myself with my very own customer sitting down before me: a man, about thirty or forty years old . . . balding . . . wearing his very own pair of try-too-hard overalls. He seemed to have had his hair—or what remained of it—quiffed into an odd shape.

It's never quite come natural for me to go about handing out *positive* comments to people; which is actually to say that it's almost against my very nature to do so. As I sat there, staring back at this neutral-expressioned man, fumbling for anything at all to say, I blurted out, "Think you should lose the hair—buzz it clean off."

The man appeared slightly startled; taken aback. As if he could only comprehend what I'd said by feeling for himself, he reached up and gently ran his palm over the quiff sculpted from his remaining hair. In a tiny, squeaky voice, he said, "All of it?"

"Uh-huh."

The man blinked several times and then got up from his seat.

Next before me was an overweight woman. She fixed me with a dead-eyed stare.

"Stop eating," I said, not even thinking about it.

She gave away no expression, and then got up from her seat.

When I glanced up, I noticed that one of the other *Truthsayers* sitting in a booth beside me was giving me a searing look. It was then that I allowed myself a smile.

This wasn't going to be that difficult at all.

6

AT THE END OF THE DAY, we were each given our personal approval rating—as rated by those who we'd 'treated'. I finished top, and passed to the next stage in which— thanking all that's holy—I was charged with scooping up another recruit for Truthsayers . . . and told, in no uncertain terms, what would happen if I didn't return in an allotted period of time.

I was given my wages for the time I'd spent at Truthsayers; and I couldn't help but notice that it was somewhere near the sum which my 'client' had first offered to bring me here.

I, though, had no intention of giving away so many credits . . . not even *half* of them. Sure, my freedom's valuable, but that doesn't mean I'm going to pay some crazy price *just because* . . .

I felt weird blasting off Truthsayers Convention with that staple still jammed into my palm; and I thought that I could feel a strange tingle passing through the surface of my skin. I knew, the credits aside, I couldn't—in good conscience—send some other hapless soul here for Truthsayers Convention to exploit.

Once I'd blasted myself free of Truthsayers Convention, I set my course for good, old Hortenine-6 where I got the staple taken out of my hand by this bespectacled mad scientist who was looking to pay his passage.

I can still recall the jovial chuckle the scientist gave when he plopped the staple—in a bloody pool—onto a table at *The Bitch's Leap* bar on Hortenine-6. I asked if he was laughing because it was really a harmless piece of scrap metal, and he told me, *No, it wasn't because of that* . . .

It was because it'd been primed to kill me within the hour if I hadn't had it forcibly removed.

I guess good things do happen to bad people, huh?

Sometimes, while rattling through space, from some sector to another, I find myself thinking about Sally, and what he might be doing now with his well-won; long-fought freedom. I can't help but wonder if he didn't just sneak his way back downstairs, to start all over again at his booth.

Some people are weird like that—unable to give up their habits whatever happens.

Whatever he was up to, I could console myself with the fact that I had shown him the way . . . what he chose to do, or not do, was entirely up to him.

AUTHOR'S NOTE

Thank you for taking the time to read one of my books. If you would like to hear about my latest releases you can sign up for my newsletter here: www.raymondsflex.com

Thanks for reading!

Raymond S Flex

Tavern Tales

An Arkle Wright Short Story Collection

Copyright © Raymond S Flex, 2014.
Published by DIB Books
All rights reserved.

Cover design and layout copyright © DIB Books, 2014.
Cover art copyright © Angela Harburn / Shutterstock, 2014.

www.ingramcontent.com/pod-product-compliance
Lightning Source LLC
Chambersburg PA
CBHW031211260626
47169CB00007B/2021